THE VISITORS IN
MRS. HALLOWAY'S BARN

THE VISITORS IN

MRS. HALLOWAY'S BARN

Thomas J. Prestopnik

PRES

To order additional copies of this book, contact:
Xlibris Corporation
1-888-7-XLIBRIS
www.Xlibris.com
Orders@Xlibris.com

CONTENTS

*Dedicated to my parents, Frances and John Prestopnik,
for their love, generosity, decency and wisdom.*

CHAPTER ONE

A Visitor In the Barn

Christopher Jordan ran as fast as a tiger through the frosty autumn leaves. He had to tell *somebody* what he had just seen, though he could hardly believe it himself.

The eleven-year-old boy raced through a field of tall, dry grass that snapped like icicles as he hurried away from the deserted barn on Mrs. Halloway's property. A cool breeze whistled by, sending falling leaves from nearby trees spinning into mini cyclones. The setting sun cast thin wobbly shadows across the landscape.

Christopher dashed across the road till he reached his house. There he spotted his younger sister Molly playing harvester on the side lawn as she always did in October. He thought himself too old for that game anymore, but Molly was only eight and still enjoyed it.

"Molly! You'll never guess what I just saw. Never in a million years!" he said, panting for breath. He pulled off a ski cap, revealing a mop of light brown hair that nearly matched the color of his eyes.

Molly glanced at her brother with a grimace. "I won't guess till you stop walking all over my tomato plants. You're squishing them, Chris. How can I harvest squished tomatoes?"

Christopher took a quick step to one side. "Better?"

"Now you're in the squash patch! I'll never finish my gardening with you around." Molly took her brother by the hand and led him where it was safer to stand.

"If you can't harvest squished tomatoes, you'll *never* be able to pick squished squash," Christopher joked.

"Very funny," Molly said, trying not to laugh, though she couldn't help grinning at her brother's silliness. She wore a purple sweatshirt jacket with the hood tied tightly about her head, but two blond ponytails still managed to peek out. "Now stay over there and talk while I gather some beans. What's so important?"

"I saw something in Mrs. Halloway's barn. Something amazing," he said. Christopher puffed air into his hands to warm them as the last rays of sunlight soaked into the ground. "Guess what it was?"

Molly shrugged. "I don't know." She and her brother occasionally used the barn as a secret hideout, though it was quite out in the open near an apple tree and therefore not very secret. Molly stopped harvesting and put her fingers to her chin as if in deep thought. "You saw a dinosaur!" she guessed, then burst out laughing.

"No! That's not a real guess, Molly. Try again, and be serious this time."

"All right, Chris." Molly thought for another moment. "I bet you saw some hay and an old wheelbarrow!" Molly bent over in a fit of giggles this time for she knew very well that those items were inside the barn.

Christopher smirked. "You're not even trying to guess, Molly."

"Oh, just tell me what you saw, Chris, if it's *that* amazing."

"All right, I will," he said, then went dead silent, hoping to build suspense. But Molly just tilted her head and clicked her tongue impatiently, so Christopher finally gave in. "I saw a king!" he said.

"You saw a *what?*"

"A king. You know, like as in *king and queen.*"

Molly sighed and went back to work in her imaginary garden. "That's a fib, Chris Jordan, and you know it. Remember what Mom and Dad said about lying—*don't!*"

"I'm not lying, Molly. I *did* see an actual king. He's in the barn, pacing back and forth. He looks really worried about something."

"And what makes you think this person is a king?"

"Because he's wearing a crown and has a sword at his side," Christopher explained. "He looks exactly like the pictures of kings Dad showed us at the museum."

Molly looked at him sternly. "Suppose I run inside and tell Mom and Dad. Then you'll probably say I made the whole story up to make me look silly."

"No I won't, Molly, because I'm telling the truth." Christopher marched off then slowly turned around. "If you don't believe me, come over and see for yourself."

"You're not going to scare me with some spider or dead mouse you found, are you?"

"Oh, your hood must be tied too tight! Of course not. Follow me and I'll show you a real king."

Molly couldn't resist the temptation any longer. So in the lingering twilight she and Christopher trudged across the field by Mrs. Halloway's house that led to the old barn. A full moon climbed in the east behind a grove of pine trees that stood tall and proud like soldiers.

"Quieter, Molly," her brother whispered. "You're making too much noise swishing all those leaves around. You'll scare the king away."

"I suppose that's the excuse you'll use when we don't find anybody in the barn."

The breeze grew stronger as they approached the two barn doors in front. They were old, weather-stained and nearly falling off their hinges. Molly stayed close to her brother but wouldn't admit she was a little frightened. The smell of damp grass danced thick in the air.

"I'm cold," Molly whispered. "Maybe we should go back before it gets too dark to see."

"Don't chicken out on me now," Christopher said, nearing the doors. Molly reluctantly followed.

He carefully opened one of the barn doors and the two slipped silently inside. The darkness smelled of hay and rotting wood.

Slowly their eyes adjusted with the help of moon rays filtering in through a window near the roof. Molly looked at the familiar surroundings; a few bales of hay, a broken-down wheelbarrow against one wall and rusty nails sticking out of the rafters. Some weeds had pushed their way up through cracks in the floor, and several wooden crates were piled near the doorway. And off at the far end of the barn below the moonlit window, Molly saw—a king!

The old man paced frantically about, unaware of the children. A brown traveling cloak was draped over his shoulders, and on top of his head of silver hair rested a delicate crown of gold. A sword hung lifelessly at his side. Molly stared with her mouth wide open till she could no longer contain her excitement.

"There *is* a king!" she burst out. "A real live king!" Her voice echoed loudly and startled the stranger.

"Who's there?" he snapped. "Make yourself known!"

Christopher and Molly walked cautiously into the moonlight. "We're Christopher and Molly Jordan. We live in the house across the road."

The king examined them closely, his eyes darting back and forth. "You are *sure* of this?"

"Of course," Molly said. "We're old enough to know who we are. But who are you?"

The king, who had a small kindly face, was taken by surprise at the question. "Who I am doesn't matter," he said hastily. "No. Not important at all."

"It matters to us," Christopher said. "You're a king after all."

The stranger's eyes widened. "A king? Why that's utter nonsense!" He laughed uncomfortably. "What a silly notion. I'm not a king."

"Yes you are."

"No I'm not!"

"But you're wearing a crown," Christopher pointed out. "And it looks expensive."

The king's eyes turned up. "So what difference does that make? Just because I choose to wear a crown doesn't mean I'm a king."

"And you have a sword at your side," Molly added.

"Well yes, but . . . "

"And that's probably a *royal* cloak draped over your shoulders," Christopher said, noting the intricate designs embroidered on it.

"Yes, I *do* have a crown and a sword and a cloak—but whether they're royal or not . . . I mean, people wear crowns all the time, right?" The stranger opened his arms as if pleading with the children. "And who *doesn't* wear a sword these days? So to say that I'm a king just because of a gold crown and a sword and a fancy cloak, well that's just, well . . . " The stranger seemed even more confused and upset as he paced frantically about the barn. "What I'm trying to say is . . . I mean, what I *want* to say is, umm . . . Oh dear. I'm not saying it very well, am I." The king plopped down on the cold ground and sighed. "All right, all right, all right. There's no use denying it. I *am* a king," he sadly admitted. "But you don't have to go out and tell the whole world! I was hoping I'd be safe from visitors in here."

Christopher noticed how miserable the king looked. "What's bothering you? I thought that being a king would be such great fun. You look like you're about to have your teeth pulled."

"*Being* a king isn't so bad," he said. "But you *know* that I'm a king. And worse, you know where I am."

"We won't tell anyone," Molly said.

The king looked up hopefully. "You mean it?"

"There's no reason we should if you don't want us to," Christopher said. "Except for our parents."

"How wonderful! I feel much safer now."

Christopher lugged over three of the wooden crates so they could all sit on them. "Just where did you come from—uh—what shall we call you?"

"King Rupert," he said, standing majestically. The moonlight danced on his silver hair. "I'm King Rupert, ruler of Endora."

"Where is that?" Christopher asked eagerly.

"Endora is a small kingdom far away from here. And right now I miss it very much."

"I don't recall learning about any place named Endora in geography class," Molly said. "How'd you get here?"

The king sat in front of the children and lowered his voice. "I don't belong to your world, Molly. I have traveled here through a magic timedoor."

"A magic timedoor! No way," she said, folding her arms to keep warm.

"Quiet, Molly," Christopher said. "If King Rupert says he came here through a timedoor, then we should believe him. After all, he *is* sitting in front of us."

"It's true," King Rupert said. "I passed through a timedoor in my kingdom which opened up into your world underneath a small bridge by a nearby river."

"There's a river not even a half mile from here. Molly and I sit on the banks and watch boats sail by."

The king smiled. "I was fortunate the timedoor opened where it did. A few feet farther ahead and I would have fallen right into the water!"

Molly laughed till Christopher nudged her with his elbow. "Why did you come here, King Rupert?" he asked.

"Shortly after I arrived in your world, the timedoor closed. So I searched the area and this barn was the first deserted place I found." The king stretched his arms and yawned. "I'm just waiting here till the door reopens."

"That's not exactly what I meant," Christopher said.

"Oh?"

"Why are you in our world? Why did you go through the timedoor in the first place?"

"Oh dear!" the king said, quickly standing. "Look how late it is. I've probably kept you up well past your bedtime. Run along now!"

"It's only after six o'clock, King Rupert. I don't go to bed till eight," Molly said. "Besides, it's Saturday tomorrow. No school."

"But maybe your parents are wondering where you are. Better go and check. Run along now!"

"We're fine right here," Christopher said, surprised that King Rupert was trying to get rid of them all of a sudden. He sensed that the king was hiding something by not answering his simple question. "Just why *is* the king here?" Christopher thought, but decided not to press him on the matter for the time being.

Christopher, Molly and King Rupert chatted for another half an hour in Mrs. Halloway's barn till Molly heard her mother calling from across the road. "*Now* it's time to go in," Molly said. "I guess we have to leave."

"Well if you must, then you must," the king said, somewhat relieved.

"Come with us!" Christopher urged. "My parents would love to meet a real king. So would little Vergil."

"He's our baby brother," Molly said.

King Rupert shook his head. "No, no, no, no, no! I'd be a dreadful inconvenience."

The children were disappointed and ready to leave when Christopher snapped his fingers. "Hang out in our cellar till we tell our parents about you. Maybe then they'll have you up for a meal."

The king admitted that he was very hungry, not having eaten since stepping through the timedoor earlier that morning. After some hesitation King Rupert agreed to the children's plan. In a short time he found himself sitting on an overturned bucket in their cold dark cellar, stuck between a box of potatoes and a sack of red and yellow apples, feeling very much alone.

Christopher and Molly, in the meantime, rushed inside to tell their parents about King Rupert just as their mother was about to call them home a second time. They chattered like squirrels as they took turns telling their story.

"A king!" Mrs. Jordan exclaimed. "In our cellar? I see the cold weather has stretched your imaginations."

"But, Mom, we're telling the truth," Christopher said. He looked at his father. "Dad, you've got to believe us! King Rupert is in our cellar this very moment. I can prove it to you."

"Very well," Mr. Jordan said, setting aside the evening paper and getting up from his reading chair. "We'll take a look if only to put an end to this game."

"I'll get little Vergil," their mother said, heading into the kitchen. The young boy sat on the floor, leaning against the humming refrigerator and pointing excitedly at the full moon outside the curtained window. "Come along, Vergil," she said, scooping him up. "We have to see the royalty your brother and sister invited into our cellar."

Mr. Jordan flipped on a light switch and the five descended the wooden cellar steps. The whistling wind could be heard outside through the dusty windows. Christopher and Molly looked around the gloomy shadows and gasped when they discovered that King Rupert had vanished.

"So where is this king of yours?" Mr. Jordan asked. "Apparently he wasn't that hungry after all."

"But he was *here*!" Molly insisted. "Maybe he had some important business to do. He seemed awfully nervous in the barn."

"I think we've had enough of kings this evening," Mrs. Jordan said as she headed back up the stairs with little Vergil. "How about a cup of hot chocolate?"

"Mother is right," Mr. Jordan said. "You kids had your joke for the night. Now up you go."

Christopher and Molly sighed and were about to head upstairs when Christopher saw something. The glimmer of a piece of metal caught the corner of his eye near the bucket where King Rupert had been sitting. "Look!" he shouted, rushing over to pick up the king's sword and crown. "King Rupert must have forgotten these when he left."

Mr. Jordan examined the items with much interest. Though he worked at a museum in the nearby city, he was very puzzled by what he saw. "I can't place these objects anywhere in history. They contain strange markings I've never seen before."

"Now do you believe us?" Molly said. "They belong to King Rupert."

"They belong to somebody, though I still find your story hard to believe."

Whether they believed it or not, Mr. and Mrs. Jordan did agree to accompany the children to Mrs. Halloway's barn to see if anyone was still there. But King Rupert was nowhere to be found. Christopher and Molly urged their parents to check down by the river bridge, hoping that the king might be searching for the magic timedoor. That idea proved unsuccessful as well.

In the end, the sword and the crown were stored in an empty apple sack in the cellar where Mrs. Jordan thought they would be out of harm's way. Mr. Jordan promised to study the objects, hoping to determine when and where in history they might have been created. And when Christopher and Molly went off to bed that night, they were very wide awake, very puzzled and very upset that King Rupert had deserted them.

CHAPTER TWO

The Second Visitor

Eleven o'clock rolled around and Christopher lay wide awake in bed. By midnight he was tossing and turning, trying to figure out why King Rupert had left the cellar. Finally he jumped out of bed, threw on his flannel bathrobe and tiptoed down the hall to Molly's room. He gently opened her door and whispered into the darkness.

"Molly. You awake?" No answer. Christopher walked to her bed and found it empty. "Molly?"

"Over here," a voice softly called. Molly sat in a chair in the corner of her room holding a stuffed koala bear. "You can't sleep either?"

Christopher sat on the edge of the bed. "No. I keep thinking about King Rupert. What a dirty trick for him to run off like that."

Molly cuddled her pet. "Even Sebastian can't get to sleep. What rotten luck! We'll probably never find another king even if we turn wrinkled and live to be forty."

Christopher agreed. "What do you think happened? Maybe he was scared off."

"I thought so too. King Rupert seemed very nervous all the time. Maybe he had an emergency to take care of."

"That's possible. And we can't forget that he left his crown and sword in our cellar. Maybe he plans to return for them soon."

"Wouldn't that be wonderful!" Molly jumped out of the chair with Sebastian. "Then we could introduce him to Mom, Dad and little Vergil."

Christopher ignored Molly's comment for his attention turned to the window near the bed. It faced towards the road outside, providing a clear view of Mrs. Halloway's barn. He studied the rickety building for a moment then looked at Molly.

"What'd you say?"

"I said it would be wonderful if King Rupert returned. But what were you looking at out the window?"

"Nothing. Thought I saw something."

"That's probably because you're up so late. Let's try to get some sleep and talk in the morning."

"Maybe you're right," Christopher said. "My brain can't keep track of all this stuff right now." But as soon as he said this, Christopher turned again to the window and stared at the barn as if a magical force drew him. "I see it this time! My eyes weren't playing tricks after all. Take a look, Molly."

Molly hurried towards the window and peered out. Mrs. Halloway's barn stood hauntingly in the moonlit field. The branches of nearby pine trees groped at the building like searching fingers. "I don't see anything," Molly said.

"Look closely between the cracks in the barn wall. I see flickers of light."

Molly strained her eyes and concentrated, then snapped to attention. "You're right, Chris! I did see a flicker of light. I really did."

Christopher searched through Molly's toybox at the base of her bed and dug out a small magnifying glass. Placing it over his eye, he gazed out the window. "This is no use," he grumbled. "Everything looks blurry."

"You look silly," Molly said. "A magnifying glass won't work for something as far away as the barn."

"If only I had a pair of binoculars."

Molly yawned, then took Sebastian and sat back down in her chair. Even the thought of a real king across the road wasn't enough to keep her awake much longer. "You won't know what's going on in the barn unless you go there yourself. But I know where I'm going now. To bed."

Christopher clapped his hands. "That's it! Let's sneak across the road to investigate."

Molly was wide awake at the suggestion. "I'm only kidding, Chris. Besides it's very cold and dark outside."

"No problem. We'll wear our slippers and jackets. Besides, we'll just be gone a few minutes. Long enough to discover what King Rupert is up to." Christopher tossed the magnifying glass into the toybox and hurried out the door. "Get ready, Molly, and meet me downstairs."

"I guess a few minutes won't hurt. Just don't wake up Mom and Dad. And especially little Vergil. If he starts to whine we'll *never* get out in secret."

But they did, as quietly as two fish through water. The children slipped out of the kitchen door into the chilly night. The moon had risen directly above. Molly shivered under her winter coat. Christopher felt just as cold but pretended not to be bothered. They hurried across the road and through the field to Mrs. Halloway's barn. The twigs and leaves on the ground crackled like a campfire as their slippered feet marched over them. Drawing nearer, they were more certain than ever that a light burned inside.

"That must be King Rupert," Christopher whispered. "Shall we find out what this is all about?" Molly nodded, and so they quietly slipped inside the barn for a second time and hid behind the pile of crates near the doors.

Their suspicions were confirmed. At the end of the barn near a small bonfire sat King Rupert. Molly wanted to rush up to him to find out why he had run off, but Christopher held her back. "Look," he said, pointing towards the fire. "There's somebody else with the king."

Then Molly saw the second figure as light from the fire shone on his face. The new stranger was a gray-haired man, many years older than King Rupert, with a beard trailing down to his waist and a hooded cloak draped over his shoulders. He was talking to the king, and Molly and Christopher listened to each word with interest.

"I'm afraid it might take a few days to determine when the door will reopen," the man said. "The star patterns here are different from those back home. Why, there's even a bright round world circling their sky. The calculations will be complicated indeed."

"How difficult?" the king inquired with a hint of fear in his voice.

"Very difficult. Especially with *him* to muddy up matters. I hope I'm up to the task."

Christopher tried to unravel the meaning of the strange conversation. He guessed that the men were talking about the timedoor King Rupert had mentioned earlier. But as to who the *him* was that King Rupert's friend referred to, Christopher hadn't the slightest idea.

Molly nudged her brother, interrupting his train of thought. "Move over a little. I want a better view."

"You can see just fine from where you are."

"No I can't," she insisted, then stood up and leaned her elbows on one of the crates piled on top of three others.

"Kneel down, Molly. They're sure to see you," Christopher warned in a stern whisper.

"King Rupert won't see us. It's too dark over here."

Molly seemed so sure of this that she stood on her tiptoes, completely exposing her face over the top of the crate. But in the next instant she felt the room start to sway, then realized that the crates she was standing on were not very sturdy. The sides of the bottom one buckled, and Molly tumbled to the ground with a scream and a crash.

"Molly!" Christopher rushed to her aid, relieved to find that she only suffered from a small bruise on her left hand and a large case of embarrassment.

"Who's there?" King Rupert's voice boomed as he jumped up

from the fire. He didn't know whether to laugh or to scold the children when he found them sprawled amidst a pile of splintered crates. Soon Christopher and Molly were warming themselves by the bonfire, explaining their little midnight adventure.

King Rupert introduced the children to his friend. His name was Artemas, the king's magician and advisor. "A real magician!" Molly said, hoping for a magic show. "Can you pull a rabbit out of a hat?"

Artemas wrinkled his brow as Christopher whispered to his sister. "I don't think he's that kind of a magician."

"I do know some magic, young lady," Artemas said, looking at her with eyes as blue as an ocean. "Though I can't recall ever pulling a rabbit out of a hat. Is that a custom for magicians in your world?"

"Some of them."

"How peculiar."

Christopher smiled then addressed King Rupert. "If I might ask, sir, why did you leave our cellar earlier? I wanted to introduce you to my parents."

The king frowned. "I'm sorry I left in a hurry."

"You even forgot to take your sword and crown," Molly said.

"Indeed I have. They were weighing me down, so I took them off for a while. All part of the burden of being a king," he said.

"But *why* did you leave?" Christopher repeated.

"While I was in your cellar I looked out of a window and saw Artemas return to the barn. I had to let him know where I was," King Rupert explained.

"I had been out examining the stars," Artemas said.

"Then you're an astronomer *and* a magician?" said Christopher in amazement.

"What's an astronomer?" the king asked.

"Someone who studies the stars and planets."

"That's exactly what I do," Artemas said. "But we magicians study the stars right along with our magic as a matter of occupation. It's all in the same bag so to speak. Am I to infer that your astronomers don't study magic?"

"Not exactly," Christopher said. "But if you're from another world, why are you studying our stars?"

"To determine when the timedoor will reopen." Artemas saw that Christopher and Molly looked confused. "When one is lucky enough to create a timedoor, one must also be careful to return through it before it closes."

"Which you obviously didn't do," Christopher said.

Artemas turned red. "I'm afraid not. An *obstacle* prevented us from returning right away, so we're stuck in your world till the door reopens."

"When will that be?"

"I'm not quite certain, which is why I was studying your sky. I know when the door will open in *my* world, but I don't know what time that corresponds to in *your* world."

Molly scratched her head, staring curiously at the magician. "I'm afraid I don't understand, Mr. Artemas. I'm only eight, after all."

"Let's see if I can make this easy to understand," he said. "From what I witnessed so far today, I've concluded that our worlds are very different. I believe a day in our world is longer than yours, as well as our year. In fact, it is winter right now in Endora and our sun is probably just rising."

"I think I see what you mean," Molly said.

"That's good," Artemas said with a smile. "Now suppose, for instance, the timedoor was to reopen at midday in four of my days. When that would be in your time I can't predict right now. But by studying the stars and the length of your day, along with the occurrences of the equinoxes and solstices—oh, and maybe throw in a nearby planet's conjunction for good measure—and then comparing them to calculations about my own world, well, *then* I should be able to find out what time it is *here* when it is a particular time *there*. Which will ultimately let me know when the timedoor will reopen." Artemas suddenly looked worried. "I only have *two* more chances."

"Why only two?" Christopher asked.

"The curious thing about a magic timedoor is that it will open and close only three times, then it is gone forever," Artemas said. "The one I created already opened and closed once. King Rupert and I have two more chances to return or we'll be trapped in your world forever."

Christopher wondered if that was the reason King Rupert had been so worried, or was there something more. He decided to pose the question he had asked earlier. "King Rupert, why did you enter our world in the first place?"

The king sat silently. He glanced at Artemas, who only shrugged his shoulders in reply. Finally King Rupert cleared his throat and addressed the children. "It seems I can't keep the truth hidden from you any longer. And since this is your world, you deserve an explanation. You see, Artemas and I went through the timedoor to—umm—hide from someone."

"Someone?" Molly asked. "Who?"

"Maybe you should start from the beginning," Artemas suggested.

"That is probably best," the king agreed, then lowered his voice as he began his tale. "Artemas and I were hiding from an evil sorcerer named Malaban who lives about a day's journey from my kingdom. He recently marched his army to my lands to attack, temporarily laying siege to my castle. Luckily my own soldiers were able to fend off Malaban's troops and turn them away. At least that's the last news I heard before I left through the timedoor. If Malaban had brought his entire guard we may not have been so fortunate."

"If your soldiers were winning, then why did you run through the timedoor?" Christopher asked.

"You would have too if you were being chased by a sorcerer who has a fancy for turning people into rocks or toads or dragonflies," the king said grimly. "Malaban was chasing me through the corridors of my castle shortly after I had spoken to my chief guard,

Ulric. He is the one who informed me that we were defeating Malaban's troops."

"Then why are you *and* Artemas here if Malaban was only chasing you?" Molly said.

"After speaking to Ulric, who had also informed me about another serious problem, I was on my way to consult with Artemas. That is when Malaban began to chase me." King Rupert's face tightened with worry and distress. "I rushed to find Artemas in his chamber, warning him to hide because Malaban was closing in fast. Since there wasn't any place to run, except back into the corridor to face the sorcerer, we escaped through a timedoor that Artemas had recently created."

"Luckily so," Artemas said with pride. "Timedoors are a hobby I work on when conditions are proper. It takes some magic on my part, but the planets have to be aligned a certain way and in the proper season. But watch out if a stray comet sweeps by. That can really complicate matters! I last created a timedoor about three years ago. It's a tricky business. You never know where a timedoor will lead. Yours is the strangest world I've been to yet. I especially like that bright satellite arcing across your sky."

"We just call it the moon," Christopher said.

"Rather a dull name, though I do wish our world had one. Still, I'm happy having seventeen planets to study in our system."

"Seventeen? We only have nine."

Artemas stroked his beard. "Only nine? A pity."

"So is that the end of your story?" Molly asked.

King Rupert jumped in. "Why yes. That's it! That's all! Entirely! Why would you think there's more? Artemas and I escaped through the timedoor and are waiting for it to reopen. Complete end of the story!" he concluded, folding his arms and not saying another word.

Christopher was intrigued by the king's eagerness to end the discussion and could get no more answers out of him. He did, however, suggest a way to help Artemas with his timedoor calculations. "My father works at a museum."

"Daddy's a crusader!" Molly said.

"A *curator*," Christopher corrected. "That's a person who runs a museum."

"How can he help?" Artemas asked.

"The museum where my dad works has a planetarium in it. That's a round room where images of the stars and planets are projected onto a domed ceiling. It's really neat," Christopher said. "He can move things around exactly like in the real sky, only much faster. Molly and I have been there lots of times for a show. Maybe you can use it to help you calculate when the timedoor will re-open."

Artemas thought this was a splendid idea and accepted Christopher's offer. Of course this meant that King Rupert and Artemas would need to meet the children's parents, and Mr. Jordan would have to agree to allow a king and a magician access to the museum, a possibility that seemed unlikely to Christopher at the moment. So the four of them walked back across Mrs. Halloway's field in the cold night air, believing that this was their best plan to return the visitors to their home so far away.

CHAPTER THREE

The Trouble With Time

"Wake up! Wake up! We have to talk with you!"

Molly and Christopher excitedly whispered this into their parents' ears as they tried to wake them up at one o'clock on a cold October morning. The children had just returned from Mrs. Halloway's barn and let King Rupert and Artemas wait downstairs in the living room.

Mrs. Jordan opened her sleepy eyes as Christopher explained what had happened. "Not again!" she said, shaking her husband awake. "Get up, Sam! The children still insist they've found a king— and now a *magician!*"

Mr. Jordan growled, his head buried in his pillow. "If you two are fibbing this time, you'll be grounded for a week! This is going too far!"

Soon the four tiptoed past little Vergil's room and marched downstairs into the living room. A single lamp was lit. Mr. and Mrs. Jordan rubbed their eyes in disbelief when seeing King Rupert and Artemas sitting on the couch. They looked at each other in shock then glared at the children.

"First you bring a stranger into our cellar, and now two are lounging in our living room. What's going on?" asked Mr. Jordan, bubbling with anger. He walked up to the strangers on his couch. "And just who are you two?"

"Didn't the children already tell you?" King Rupert kindly inquired.

"They mentioned something about a king and a magician. And though your friend with the long beard might pass for a magic man," Mr. Jordan said, rolling his eyes, "I'm afraid you look nothing like a king!"

"Don't forget the crown and the sword," Molly said.

"Of course," King Rupert agreed. "I would look more like a king if I had them."

Mr. Jordan had forgotten about those items and calmed down. Hadn't he admitted that the sword and crown were genuine? "But I still find it difficult to believe you're an actual king—crown or no crown. Can you prove it?"

King Rupert was unprepared for such a challenge. No one had ever doubted his word before. All the power he had attained in Endora would amount to nothing if he had to remain in this world forever. "I might tell you stories about my kingdom, but you could say I was lying. So I guess that isn't the type of proof you're looking for."

"Not really," Mr. Jordan said.

Molly pleaded with her father. "Why don't you believe him, Daddy?"

"Because I'm wide awake and miserable in the middle of this cold night. That's one reason," Mr. Jordan said. He noticed that his wife had sat on one of the living room chairs and was half asleep. "And look at your mother! This whole matter could have waited till morning. And to top things off—" But Mr. Jordan stopped speaking when he noticed little Vergil walking quietly into the room in his pajamas, clutching a stuffed teddy bear. "Now we've wakened Vergil besides. And you want me to believe them?"

"Don't be too harsh, Sam," Mrs. Jordan said wearily. "Maybe they are who they claim. That crown looked very royal to me."

"All right," he said with a hint of challenge in his voice. "Maybe our king here can't prove himself to be a real king." He pointed a finger at Artemas. "But you, sir, should certainly have no problem proving yourself a magician. Show us some magic!"

Mr. Jordan sat next to his wife. Christopher, Molly and little Vergil were now eager and wide awake, taking seats on the floor in anticipation of a genuine magic show.

"I should have thought of that myself," Artemas said. "What a wonderful idea! Now what should I do?"

"Make an elephant appear in the room!" Molly said.

"No smelly elephants in the house!" shouted her father. "That goes for rhinos and hippos too!"

"Change all the leaves in the backyard into gold," Christopher suggested.

"That idea I like," Mr. Jordan said.

"All very good suggestions, but something simple should do the trick." Artemas walked over to a coffee table on one side of the room. A bowl of decorative green and purple grapes rested on top. "Do you all see these?"

"They're plastic grapes," Molly said.

"Let me guess," muttered Mr. Jordan sarcastically. "You're going to turn them into *real* grapes? Hardly a convincing trick. You might have switched them while we were upstairs."

"I did no such thing. My trick is better."

All sat eagerly as the magician backed a few steps away from the coffee table. Everyone kept their eyes on the bowl of plastic grapes. Then Artemas raised his hands, mumbled a few incantations, then pointed his fingers sharply at the bowl crying *findelgundygro*!—but nothing happened. He tried a second time with the same results.

"Some magician," Mr. Jordan said with a smirk.

"My powers seem a tad rusty," said a puzzled Artemas. "How odd. Please let me try one more time." The magician gritted his teeth and squinted his eyes as he concentrated, mumbled a few more words, then waved his hands as quick as a bird in flight. "Findelgundygro!" he commanded.

Suddenly a sprawling, leafy, sweet-smelling grapevine sprouted out of the fruit bowl and branched off, some shoots taking root in the floor as others climbed up the walls and across the ceiling.

Green fleshy leaves bloomed everywhere, covering the living room with a rich and wondrous canopy. Soon glistening bunches of green and purple grapes popped out along the curling vines, the largest, sweetest and most delicious grapes that the Jordan family had ever tasted.

Christopher and Molly ran in and out and around the leafy branches, laughing and chasing each other. Even little Vergil joined in the act, squealing hysterically as he jumped up and down in an attempt to grab a huge cluster of grapes hanging above him. Mr. and Mrs. Jordan were as delighted as their children, walking hand in hand through the grapevine in wonderment. All doubts about the visitors were dispelled.

Artemas was equally pleased with his performance, and it took King Rupert several minutes to bring everyone back to their senses. "Please sit down. We still have a big problem to solve!"

In the end, Artemas cast another spell to make the grapevine disappear, though this took as much effort as it did to create it. He couldn't understand why. The children even gathered enough grapes to fill a dozen large bowls. Mrs. Jordan suspected that she would be making grape juice and jam till Christmas.

With the excitement over, King Rupert again related his tale of the timedoor. Molly and Christopher listened attentively, though they had heard it all before. Their parents were fascinated with details about the magic door, the sorcerer Malaban and his invading troops, and the fact that there were only two chances remaining for King Rupert and Artemas to return to Endora.

Mr. Jordan interrupted the king at one point. "Correct me if I'm wrong, but didn't you say that you and Artemas ran through the timedoor because Malaban was chasing after you?"

"That's correct," said King Rupert.

"Well, if a sorcerer was chasing after me and I had a magician handy, why not simply confront the sorcerer and have the magician deal with him properly?"

King Rupert turned pale. "Do you know what you're saying?"

Artemas took it upon himself to answer Mr. Jordan's question. "You need to understand the difference between a magician and a sorcerer. I do have some magical powers, but compared to a sorcerer, why—there *is* no comparison! My spells and illusions are no match to what a sorcerer can do, especially one as crafty as Malaban." Artemas shuddered at the thought of a confrontation between himself and Malaban. "I had no choice but to flee with my king."

"I had no idea this Malaban fellow was so powerful," Mrs. Jordan said. "Why did he attack your kingdom? How much power can one person want?"

King Rupert wrung his hands. "Malaban attacked us because— that's what evil sorcerers *do*, I suppose. Who can see into the mind of a person like that? But Malaban wasn't always evil."

"He wasn't?" Molly climbed on her father's lap to listen to the rest of the story.

"Malaban was once a magician like Artemas," the king explained. "A good person, loyal to King Alexander in lands not far from Endora. Malaban was also fond of traveling, and years ago met a sorcerer in unexplored lands. Malaban learned some of his magic, and his powers grew tremendously. When he returned to his king, Malaban seemed quite the same magician he always was. For a while anyway."

"Then what happened?" Mrs. Jordan asked, holding little Vergil who was fast falling asleep.

"Unfortunately Malaban began to excel in the magic he had learned. He grew so powerful that his mind was twisted, turning him away from all that was good. All he desired was more power over other people. He was able to turn some of King Alexander's men to his own side, and also recruited scores of trolls and goblins from the nearby mountains. In time they seized the king's castle and his entire kingdom, banishing King Alexander into the wilderness. But that wasn't enough for Malaban. His appetite for power still grows." King Rupert shuddered. "He craves even more land to spread his evil. That is why he attacked my kingdom.

Though my troops defeated his army once, I fear he may attack my castle again in greater numbers. I must get back to Endora to stop him!"

King Rupert's story moved Mr. Jordan, and he offered to assist the king in any way possible. When Christopher mentioned using the planetarium in the museum in order to determine when the timedoor would reopen, his father agreed that it was an excellent idea. Mr. Jordan would take Artemas there at once so he could begin his calculations.

"Now will be the best time to go. There'll be nobody around to bother us or to get suspicious," he said.

King Rupert thanked Mr. Jordan again and again. "I'm beginning to feel there is some hope after all."

Mr. Jordan drove King Rupert and Artemas to the museum in the city that very hour. Mrs. Jordan allowed Christopher and Molly to tag along since tomorrow was Saturday and there would be no school. After parking the car, Mr. Jordan led them through a back door. He turned off the museum alarm system, then guided them through the shadowy hallways.

The floors were made of smooth glassy tiles that looked like dark rich marble. A series of narrow windows on the right stretched all the way to the ceiling. Moonlight streamed through, bouncing off the slick floor and dancing on the glass display cases against another wall.

"Luckily there's a full moon tonight. We'll have plenty of light to reach the planetarium," Mr. Jordan said.

"Everything feels spooky," Molly whispered, staying close to her father as they walked. Their footsteps echoed through the vast chambers of the building.

"This is even more fun than playing in Mrs. Halloway's barn!" Christopher said.

"We're not here to have fun," his father reminded him. "We have serious work to do. Remember that."

When they at last reached the planetarium, the group milled about as Mr. Jordan searched for the correct key to unlock the door. King Rupert wandered a few steps and glanced down an adjacent corridor, then froze in fear. "Oh my!" he whispered, running back to the others. "The enemy has discovered us! We must leave at once."

Christopher and Molly grabbed the king's arm as he tried to flee, holding him back till their father could figure out what was troubling him. "There's nothing to be afraid of in here," Molly assured him.

"But I saw him in that hallway!" the king insisted. "We are doomed! Now I shall never get home."

After some convincing from Mr. Jordan, King Rupert was persuaded to take a closer look down the corridor. Artemas and the children stood at his side. To his relief, the only enemy waiting there was an ancient suit of knight's armor, though Christopher admitted it did look sinister in the dim light.

"I told you there was nothing to be afraid of," Molly said. "Who did you think it was?"

"Why—nobody, of course!" King Rupert snapped. "My eyes played a trick on me. Let's forget it and move on."

All agreed, though Christopher thought there was more to the king's behavior than he let on. "I still think King Rupert is hiding something," Christopher whispered to his father. "He's still as jittery as he was in the barn."

Mr. Jordan turned on the lights in the planetarium, allowing everyone to find a seat while he went to the control panel. The large circular room had a white domed ceiling and two rings of comfortable cushioned chairs. With everyone in place, Mr. Jordan dimmed the lights till the room was bathed in blackness. Molly couldn't even see her brother, though he sat right next to her. King Rupert and Artemas sat in the row behind them. All gazed up at the ceiling, watching, waiting. Then it happened.

The stars appeared slowly, dull and dim, then grew to bright shining dots like white hot coals. Soon all of the northern constellations were alive and spinning. The Milky Way band splashed across the ceiling. Pegasus and Andromeda took center stage. And there was Orion with his sword. Mars loomed with a fiery redness, and Venus was white as snow. The sun, moon and stars rose and set again and again as the days became seconds. All watched with giddy fascination, forgetting where they were and for what reason, only pleased that the heavens honored them with such a spectacular performance.

A gentle voice beckoned the stargazers back to reality. "Will this help you?" Mr. Jordan asked, standing at the controls. "Artemas, will this help you?"

"What?" the magician asked as if awakened from a trance. "Oh yes, it should help a great deal." Artemas straightened up in his chair. "I seem to have been lost in thought. What an amazing invention you have here."

"I'll bet your timedoor is even more amazing," Christopher said.

"It does have its charm," he admitted. "Now I'll have to study your sky much more carefully than in that first demonstration."

"That will be no problem," Mr. Jordan said. "We can control the rising and setting of the sun and stars at any speed you'd like. I also have other star charts and astronomical tables to aid in your calculations."

"Will your work take very long, Artemas?" the king asked anxiously.

"Several hours at least. I never had to do this before. Never got stuck in another world," he said, a bit embarrassed.

"Well hurry if you can. I must find out what's happening in my castle. I must save my people! I must save my *daughter*!" he cried, then went silent, realizing too late the words he had spoken.

Molly turned to the king. "Why didn't you tell us you had a daughter? Is she in trouble?"

King Rupert sat quietly for a few moments and took a deep breath. "Yes. I do have a daughter. Rosalind is her name. She is very young and very beautiful. I didn't speak of her before because I didn't want to cause any unnecessary worry. And yes," he said, his voice trembling, "she is in trouble. A lot of trouble."

"In what way?" Mr. Jordan asked as he gathered up a small pile of star charts.

"I might as well tell you now," the king said. "Do you remember when I mentioned that Ulric, my chief guard, told me that we were winning against Malaban's army?"

"Yes," said Christopher. "You said Malaban's troops had left your castle."

"Ulric, however, had other news for me which I neglected to tell you," King Rupert continued sadly. "Ulric told me that Malaban's retreating soldiers had kidnapped my daughter Rosalind and were taking her back to their fortress. That's why I ran to get Artemas. I needed his help. But since Malaban was chasing me soon after, the two of us had no choice but to flee through the timedoor." King Rupert wiped a tear from his eye. "I feel so helpless and miserable. I've deserted my daughter when she needs me most. She must think I'm a complete failure."

"Nonsense!" Molly said. "You had no choice but to run away. If you faced Malaban, he might have turned you into something dreadful. Then you would *never* be able to save Rosalind."

Christopher agreed. "At least now you can put up a good fight. We just have to get you back to Endora first."

"Thank you for being so understanding," the king said. "You've been more help than I deserve."

Artemas and Mr. Jordan immediately went to work to determine when the timedoor would reopen. King Rupert watched in silence, pacing the room now and then as the two men studied star charts and numerical tables and scribbled out page-long calculations. Occasionally they took some observations of the stars and planets projected onto the planetarium ceiling.

Molly and Christopher waited in the hallway, not wanting to bother the others. The corridor was dark and shadowy, looking like a long empty cave at this time of night. Their thin whispers echoed off the walls.

"Do you think King Rupert's daughter is all right, Chris? I think it's terrible that she was kidnapped by a mob of horrible soldiers." Molly sat on the floor with her back to the wall and her legs bent, resting her chin on her knees. She yawned. Christopher sat next to her.

"I hope she's okay. I'll be steaming if that sorcerer Malaban hurts her," Christopher said. He thought for a moment. "I wonder if anyone rescued her yet. Do you think so?" He waited for a reply. "Molly. Molly, do you—?" Christopher glanced at his sister and noticed she had fallen asleep. He removed his jacket and draped it over her, and very soon after, though he tried his best not to, Christopher fell asleep too.

They were awakened an hour or so before dawn by their father. The children stretched and yawned before recalling where they were. "The timedoor!" Christopher said when realizing he was still in the museum. "Where's King Rupert and Artemas? They didn't leave, did they?"

"They're hiding out in the museum basement," Mr. Jordan said. "This way I'll be able to look in on them."

"Does that mean that Artemas couldn't figure out when the timedoor will reopen?" Molly asked.

"Not at all. Artemas figured out everything! He said the door will reopen next Saturday, a week from today, right at sunrise. They'll be going home very soon," Mr. Jordan said delightedly. "Very soon."

CHAPTER FOUR

Return To Endora

The week turned gray, cold and wet, making time crawl along like a snail across a garden. Blustery rains pasted orange and yellow leaves onto the roads and lawns. Molly and Christopher sat in agony at their desks in school, required to read and write and figure out math problems, when all they really wanted to think about was the timedoor. They couldn't wait to help King Rupert and Artemas return home, wanting so much to see how a magical timedoor worked. Though the children never told anyone, they both secretly desired to see Endora for themselves.

Then like magic itself, the rains ceased and Saturday finally rolled around. Since Artemas figured out that the timedoor would reopen at sunrise, he, King Rupert and the entire Jordan family drove down to the river half an hour before the sun peeked over the horizon to wait. They wanted plenty of time to spare before the magical event.

It was a damp and misty morning, chilling to the bone. King Rupert insisted several times that they needn't stand right at the bridge till sunrise, so Mrs. Jordan suggested that they wait in a nearby diner. "A hot cup of coffee would taste wonderful right now."

The group of seven walked over to the diner situated between the river and the road. The brown clapboards on the building were badly chipped and peeling, and the windows were grimy and cracked. But it was toasty warm inside and all were grateful for that as they slid into a booth. Mr. Jordan ordered hot chocolate for the children and coffee for himself and his wife. King Rupert and Artemas weren't in the mood to drink anything at the moment.

Since they were the only customers in the place, they were served right away by Mr. Smithers, who owned the diner. He was a rumpled looking man, with his hair uncombed and his face unshaven. He didn't say much, though was quite curious as to why such a strange looking group was down by the river so early in the morning. He was happy for their business nonetheless, since he rarely had many customers anymore. After serving their drinks, Mr. Smithers pretended to wipe off the counter by the cash register as he tried to listen to their conversation.

King Rupert kept looking out of the door, trying to get a glimpse of the bridge through the mist. "I appreciate all the help you've given us," he said. "But it isn't really necessary for you to wait here till we leave. Why don't you all go home and get some sleep."

"Nonsense," Mr. Jordan said. "We've seen you this far through your ordeal, so we won't abandon you now."

"That's kind, but you really *don't* have to stay."

It seemed to Christopher as if King Rupert didn't want them around, though he hoped it was only his imagination. "We'll be with you to the very end."

"Oh, if you must," he sadly said.

Mr. Smithers heard all of this and was greatly intrigued, though he was unable to make any sense out of it. "What a strange bunch," he thought. "I wonder what they're up to?"

As the minutes ticked away, King Rupert grew more glum and uneasy. Artemas was quiet as well. Then the king's eyes lit up. "Dear me! After all this time I still don't have my crown and sword. I can't return without them."

"They're still in the apple sack in our cellar," Mrs. Jordan said. "I'll drive home and get them at once. You wouldn't be a proper king without those."

"Good idea," the king hastily agreed. "Take the whole family with you. Artemas and I will wait here."

"That's not necessary," Mr. Jordan said. "I'll go home and get the items myself. I'll only be a minute."

Before King Rupert could say another word, Mrs. Jordan decided that she and little Vergil would accompany him. "The weather is so damp down here that I want to get Vergil a heavier jacket. Do you kids want to come along too and grab some warmer clothes?"

"A marvelous idea!" the king said.

"We'll be fine, Mom," Molly said.

"We'd rather stay here with King Rupert and Artemas," Christopher added. "We've been waiting for this day the entire week."

"Very well," she said. "Your father and I will return in a few minutes. Behave now."

Molly and Christopher were thrilled to wait in the diner on their own, though the king and Artemas were less than enthusiastic. As the minutes passed, King Rupert grew more and more agitated. He looked as fidgety as a hamster in a cage. The children sensed that something troubled their friend, but kept quiet about it after receiving a stern glance from Artemas. When it appeared that King Rupert was ready to burst, he promptly stood up and took a deep breath.

"I need a dose of fresh air. Artemas, I want you to accompany me. You children wait here," the king commanded. "Good-bye," he softly added, walking out of the diner with the magician. Mr. Smithers, who had been watching all the while, quietly slipped out through the back door.

Molly shook her head in wonder. "Now isn't that the oddest thing, Christopher. King Rupert acts as nervous as on the night we found him in Mrs. Halloway's barn."

"I've noticed it too. There's something he's holding back from us, but I just can't place my finger on it."

Molly sipped her hot chocolate. "And did you notice how he said good-bye to us? He sounded as if he'd never see us again."

A horrible thought ran through Christopher's mind at that instant. He looked at Molly with a frightful stare. "You don't suppose—!" he began, when Mr. Smithers rushed inside through the back door. He went to the children's booth and sat down, completely out of breath.

"Pardon me for intruding," he managed to say between gasps for air, "but I overheard your two friends outside."

Molly raised her eyebrows. "Overheard?"

"Okay! Okay! So I spied on them. It's my diner after all, and they both seem kind of the odd type if you ask me. I mean, check out those outfits they're wearing. Where'd you find those two? In a bargain Halloween shop?"

"What did they say?" Christopher asked.

"Weird things. The one with the beard kept saying that there wasn't much time. Something about a door closing at any minute." Mr. Smithers grabbed one of the mugs of coffee on the table and took a deep gulp. "Excuse me for helping myself, but I needed that!" He wiped his mouth on his sleeve. "Yuck. It tastes awful!"

"Go on. What else?" Christopher asked, drumming his hands on the table.

"They said they needed to get away without being discovered. By who, I'm not sure. Or is it by *whom*? I always got those two mixed up. Do you? Owls never have that problem."

"Who cares, mister! What else did they say?"

"The name is Mr. *Smithers*, young man, and I'll tell you exactly what else they said." Then he scratched his head sheepishly. "Well, umm, actually they didn't *say* anything else. I followed them to the bridge though, but lost them in the mist. I rushed back here hoping you two could tell me what's going on. As much as I hate this rundown place, I don't want any shenanigans in my diner."

Christopher assured him that nothing would happen to the diner, then he said a quick good-bye and dashed outside. Molly chased after him. They had only run a few yards through the wet grass along the misty river when Molly demanded that they stop.

"You're rushing so fast, Chris, that I can't catch my breath! Slow down. Where are you going in such a hurry? We're supposed to wait for Mom and Dad at the diner. What's going on?"

"Don't you know?" her brother said. "I just figured it out. King Rupert and Artemas have already left through the timedoor. It'll probably close up any second."

"That's ridiculous!" Molly crossed her arms. "Artemas said that the door won't even *open* until sunrise. That's still a few minutes away."

Christopher knew he didn't have time to stand there trying to convince his sister, so he ran to the bridge as he talked, with Molly chasing after him. "Artemas lied about the door! He said it would *open* at sunrise. But after what Mr. Smithers overheard, I think the timedoor will *close* at sunrise! It must be open right now. King Rupert didn't want us to know that."

"But why?" shouted Molly.

Christopher only shrugged as he ran. At last they arrived at the bridge which was barely visible as it extended across the river. White mists curled around its gray metal beams, coating them with droplets of icy water. Christopher and Molly walked along the river bank till they were underneath the bridge near a stone wall support.

"They're not here!" Christopher punched his hand, angry and saddened that King Rupert and Artemas had deserted them. "And after all the help we gave them." He sat down in the wet grass and leaned against the stone wall. "I just can't believe it . . . "

Molly was as crushed as her brother and wanted to go home and forget the entire week. She took her brother's hand, trying to get him to stand up. "Let's go, Chris. There's nothing we can do now." But Christopher wouldn't budge as Molly tugged on his arm. "We're just going to freeze here if we—" Molly went silent. Her mouth opened wide in surprise as her brother's hand slipped out of her own. She pointed to a section of the stone wall a few feet to the left of her brother. "Look at *that*, Chris!"

A slight breeze had stirred up some of the mist under the bridge, exposing part of the stone wall. That section appeared wavy and weak like the steamy air above a hot asphalt road in summertime. The surrounding stone was solid. Christopher noticed it too and jumped to his feet. He carefully pressed his fingers against the wall and slowly moved them over towards the section Molly had spotted. He yelped like a frightened pup when his hand disappeared through the stone.

"The timedoor! It's still open, Molly! We have to follow King Rupert if we're ever going to find out what's really going on. We have to hurry before it closes."

Molly's spirits soared. She wanted to rush through the timedoor at once, then remembered one simple fact. "We can't leave. Mom and Dad won't know what happened to us."

"No problem." Christopher found a small rock lying nearby and scrawled a message on the stone near the timedoor. WE FOLLOWED KING RUPERT AND ARTEMAS TO ENDORA. WE'LL BE BACK WHEN THE TIMEDOOR OPENS AGAIN. LOVE MOLLY AND CHRIS. He drew an arrow indicating where the door opened, then tossed the stone into the river. "Mom and Dad will eventually search for us here. They'll know we're okay."

"I suppose," Molly said timidly, beginning to have second thoughts. "Do you think it's safe?"

"King Rupert and Artemas arrived in our world in one piece, so I'm certain we'll be fine too," her brother assured her. "What do you say, Molly? It's now or never."

Molly glanced at the timedoor, then nodded confidently. "Let's go, Chris! We won't get a chance like this again."

After taking a deep breath, Christopher stepped through the timedoor and Molly followed, clutching his hand like a vice. In an instant all went as black as coal, then slowly, thousands upon thousands of stars appeared all around them. They felt a solid path beneath their feet, but could see nothing holding them up. All was a dizzying and magical whirlpool of stars.

"I feel like I'm walking in space," Molly said. "I'm a little bit scared, yet for some reason I know everything will turn out just fine."

Christopher moved them along. "Keep walking. I think the door was starting to close after we entered. It appeared to be getting more solid around the edges. I can't imagine what would happen if it closed completely while we were still inside." The thought scared Molly too, so she quickened her pace.

The stars faded as they neared the other end, and the blackness slowly dissolved into grays and whites. After four or five more steps, Christopher and Molly emerged through another stone wall into a small stuffy room lit by several drooping candles and a few burning logs crackling away in a fireplace. They turned around and saw the faint outline of the timedoor still visible.

"This must be Artemas' chamber," Christopher guessed. "Let's see if we can find King Rupert." They opened a door and peered out into an empty corridor. Blazing torches hung from the smooth stone walls, sending wisps of smoke to the high ceiling. There was dead silence.

Molly suddenly spun around. "I thought I heard someone behind us!"

The children stepped back into the magician's chamber and looked about. A table near the fireplace overflowed with stone jars and glass vials of colorful liquids, powders and potions. Shelves of parchment scrolls lined the room. There was even a coat tree near the empty stone wall where they had entered. Piles and piles of cloaks and scarves were hung on it, and several pairs of large boots were crowded around the base. All in all, every object appeared well used and stuffed snugly into place. A set of double doors, opposite the door leading into the corridor, was slightly ajar.

"There's nobody else in here," Christopher assured Molly. "You're imagining things."

But as soon as he uttered that last word, a deafening crack stung their ears like a clap of thunder. The glass vials on the table rattled. Though fearing the worst, they soon discovered what had happened. The bare wall near the coat tree now appeared cold and gray, the stone as solid as iron. The timedoor had closed.

"I guess we're trapped here for a while," Christopher said. "So we might as well have a look around."

Before stepping out into the hallway again, the children decided to look behind the double doors. The one on the right was partially open, letting in a cool draft. Christopher opened it wide, making the candles flicker and the flames in the fireplace dance wildly.

The doors led onto a large stone balcony overlooking the lands to the north. It was a winter day in Endora as the sun climbed across the cloudy gray sky. Christopher estimated that it was probably midday. Very little snow covered the vast brown patches of ground that stretched out as far as they could see.

Molly walked over to the low fence around the balcony and looked down. "Chris, we must be a million feet high!"

The children realized they stood in one of the uppermost chambers in the castle. Christopher wondered why Artemas needed a balcony overlooking the kingdom, then soon discovered the answer. Off to one side stood a bulky object covered by a heavy piece of canvas. Christopher lifted a corner and saw a crudely made telescope underneath.

"So Artemas studies the stars after all," he concluded, realizing what a spectacular view of the sky the magician would have from this vantage point. He replaced the canvas over the telescope to keep it safe from the cold.

"Let's get inside again. I'm freezing," Molly said, her teeth chattering.

So they warmed themselves by the fire for a few minutes before daring to leave the magician's chamber. Then gathering up their courage, they stepped out into the corridor to begin their search for King Rupert and Artemas.

This proved to be quite a task. The upper corridors of the castle were deserted and seemed like a maze. For several minutes the children traveled in circles. Not even a guard was spotted who might give them some help. But since they were trespassing, Christopher thought he and Molly were better off not being seen until they found the king. In time, Molly discovered a stairway that led to the lower levels of the castle.

Soon voices could be heard, but not having any idea which direction they were coming from, Christopher decided that they should look inside every door, one corridor at a time. If a guard should approach, the children agreed to hide out in the nearest empty room. So the monotonous game of search-for-the-king continued.

In the next half hour, Christopher and Molly looked inside at least thirty rooms, dodged six guards and even managed to indulge in a snack of dried bread, fruit and water in one of the unoccupied kitchens. Soon they rounded a corner which led to a wide stone passageway with several more doors on each side. Christopher checked the doors on one side and Molly did the same on the other. After a glance into one of her rooms, Molly quickly closed the door and called her brother.

"Chris! Hurry! I think I found it!"

Christopher dashed across the corridor and Molly carefully reopened the door. A small tunnel-like archway stretched along for about twenty feet, opening up into a large chamber. Since there were no torches along the tunnel walls, the children were able to sneak inside and observe, undetected in the shadows.

The circular chamber was lined around the perimeter with tall marble pillars. Torches fastened to each pillar cast away much of the gloom that seemed a common sight in the rest of the castle. In the center was a long oak table, with many of the king's soldiers seated on either side. At the head of the table, farthest from where the children were hiding, sat King Rupert. Ulric, the king's chief guard, sat at the opposite end. Artemas was on the king's left, and to his right, sitting primly but with a look of dismay, was King Rupert's wife, Queen Eleanor.

"I see he made it back safely," Christopher whispered sarcastically.

"We should march right out there and demand to know why he ran away from us!" Molly said.

"Let's listen to what they have to say first. Maybe we'll learn something about the sorcerer who attacked his castle."

As Christopher suspected, the meeting concerned the recent invasion by Malaban. They heard that the king's daughter, Rosalind, had been kidnapped by Malaban's soldiers before they retreated. What surprised Christopher and Molly most was that none of King Rupert's men had any idea where Malaban himself had gone. Since the sorcerer hadn't left Endora with his own army, his whereabouts were a mystery. A few of the king's soldiers suggested that their army should attack Malaban's fortress at once and rescue Princess Rosalind. But as much as King Rupert wanted to do that, he immediately dismissed the idea.

"You forget that we defeated Malaban's army because he didn't send all of his troops. Overconfidence on his part. However, if we attack now we shall be greatly outnumbered. We wouldn't stand a chance." King Rupert sighed and held his wife's trembling hand. "If I am to save our dear Rosalind, it will have to be done in secret and with few people. That is the only way."

All were silent. The king had made up his mind, so there seemed nothing left to discuss. Everyone patiently waited to hear the details of King Rupert's plan, but he remained quiet as if in deep thought. Christopher and Molly couldn't stand waiting in the dark tunnel for another instant, so they decided to confront the king.

"It's about time we get some answers," Christopher said. "It's about time *we* ask the questions!"

Gathering up every bit of courage they possessed, Christopher and Molly emerged out of the shadows and into the circle of pillars, marching right up to King Rupert's side. The astonishment on his face rendered him speechless. Queen Eleanor and the soldiers, though, were quite amused at the two determined strangers barging into their midst.

"What is the meaning of this?" King Rupert finally managed to sputter. "You children follow me like my own shadow. Why are you here? *How* are you here?"

"You lied to us!" Christopher said, throwing a glance at Artemas too. "You ran away from the diner without so much as an explanation. Is that how you thank us for all our help?"

The king was speechless once again and quite ashamed of himself. As all eyes were on him, he knew it wouldn't be to his advantage to discuss the matter here. So he briefly explained the children's presence, then dismissed everyone except Queen Eleanor, Artemas and Ulric.

Before Christopher could spout another word, King Rupert introduced his wife, if only to gain some time to think. "This is my lovely wife, Queen Eleanor of Endora."

"Pleased to meet you, ma'am," Molly said. She curtsied, feeling it was the proper thing to do.

"Hi," Christopher said, almost blushing. Somehow meeting royalty in a castle rather than in a barn seemed a much more sobering experience.

"I am pleased to meet both of you," Queen Eleanor said. "Yet my husband has never mentioned you before," she added, glancing suspiciously at King Rupert.

The king cleared his throat nervously. "You see, dear, I hadn't planned on ever seeing these children again. It seems I was quite wrong." He briefly told Queen Eleanor of his encounter with Malaban and the escape through the timedoor, then addressed the children. "Forgive me and Artemas for running off without saying good-bye. I wish I could tell you more, but I simply can't."

"You mean you *won't*," Christopher said. "And even if you don't tell us why you left, you won't get rid of us so easily. The timedoor closed right after we walked through. Now we're stuck in your world for a time."

The king's eyes lit up. "It's closed? How wonderful! That means it will only open up to your world one more time. We're safe for now."

The children didn't know what the King had meant by that remark, so Christopher decided to pose a question to Artemas. "When will the timedoor reopen?"

"In about six days. Now that I'm back home, the calculations are quite simple."

"Is that in six of your days or six of our days?"

"Six of my days," Artemas said.

Christopher thought for a moment then whispered into Molly's ear. She nodded happily and encouraged her brother to tell the king. "Since Molly and I will be here for a while, we have only one thing to ask of you." King Rupert looked puzzled but signaled for him to go on. "Since we did so many favors for you and Artemas in our world, Molly and I think it fair that you allow us one favor in return."

"That sounds reasonable," the king said after seeing Queen Eleanor nod her head in approval. "I'll grant you any request, so long as you don't ask for possession of my kingdom."

"Do you promise to keep your word?" Molly asked.

"My word of honor!" King Rupert said. "I am a king after all. If I make a promise I stick to it. If I didn't, why, that would be very, well—unkingly! Isn't that right, dear?" he added, patting her hand.

"We'll find out shortly," the queen said with a smile. "My husband is usually one to keep his word."

"That's all we wanted to hear," Christopher said. "Then this is our request. Molly and I wish to go with you when you rescue Princess Rosalind from Malaban's fortress. We offer our services which you can't refuse, for that is the favor we are asking."

King Rupert slapped a hand to his forehead. "Isn't there anything else you'd rather have? A pile of gold and diamonds perhaps? How about a dozen prized horses?"

"We've made our choice," Molly said. "Besides, you mentioned that you only wanted a few people to make the rescue. Who would ever suspect kids like us to be involved in such a thing?"

This proved to be an excellent point, yet still the king wasn't satisfied. Before Christopher and Molly had interrupted the meeting, King Rupert was about to announce who would accompany him on the rescue attempt. He would go, along with Artemas,

Ulric and two of Ulric's best soldiers. The king thought five men would be sufficient. But now that the children had cornered him into a promise, King Rupert decided, as painful as it was, to allow Christopher and Molly to go in place of the two soldiers. Christopher hooted in delight and Molly grinned, telling King Rupert to cheer up. She insisted that two children might prove to be of more help than anyone could ever imagine.

CHAPTER FIVE

A Spy On the Plains

The rescue party gathered in King Rupert's chamber early that evening to hear his plan. They would leave for Malaban's fortress that very night under the cover of darkness. Christopher and Molly were unprepared for so sudden a departure, especially in the dead of a chilly winter night. Being included in the rescue suddenly grew less attractive.

"We'll travel on horseback, and if we're lucky, our journey should take only a day," the king said. "We'll camp out on the plains, keep our meals brief and our conversation to a minimum. Hopefully only the wind and the grass will know of our plans."

Christopher raised his hand. "Who are we trying to hide from? Surely we don't have to worry about being watched, at least not until we near Malaban's castle."

Ulric stepped forward, his muscular arms and wind-burned face a testament to many grueling adventures in the king's service. "Always be on the lookout for your enemy," he warned. "Even though we are a day's journey from our destination, spies can lurk everywhere. *Always* be on guard."

"I'll remember that," Christopher said.

The talk of spies, in addition to a late start, put a damper on the children's spirits. Now more than ever they wished they hadn't invited themselves along. But they couldn't turn their backs at the first sign of discomfort, so Christopher and Molly kept their thoughts private. They just wanted to begin their trek at once in order to end it as soon as possible.

So several hours before midnight, King Rupert kissed Queen Eleanor good-bye and told her not to worry. "We shall find Rosalind and bring her back safely. I give you my word."

"Please be careful," she said, trying to smile. "I'll count the minutes till you return."

Everyone loaded food and supplies onto their horses and departed solemnly across the castle drawbridge under a canopy of gray and black clouds. Ulric rode in the lead, followed by King Rupert and Artemas, who traveled side by side, consulting in whispers along the way. Christopher and Molly trailed behind on the same horse, bundled up in fur-lined coats to protect them from the bitter winds sweeping across the plains. They couldn't imagine what adventures awaited them.

The five traveled several miles north of the castle in the first few hours. The clouds had scattered by then, exposing thousands of bright stars above. Silhouettes of sharp rocky mountains loomed off to their left as the horses trotted over dried stalks of grass that brushed harshly against one another in a biting breeze. The barrenness of this winter world depressed Christopher. He longed to see a shining silver moon climb over the horizon.

"Don't tell the others, Chris, but I wish I was back home," Molly whispered. "I'm cold, tired and quite sure it's way past my bedtime. Maybe it wasn't such a bright idea to come along after all."

"Maybe, but it's too late to turn back. We promised to help, so now we have to keep our word no matter how bad things get," he said. "Hopefully we'll stop to rest soon. I'm tired too."

Molly wanted so much to close her eyes, but the uneven gait of the horse chased away any chance for sleep. The ground was hard and uneven, sloping gently at times or climbing so steeply that the children nearly fell off their horse. Both were quite hungry too, neither having eaten anything since the small snack of bread, fruit and water in the castle. They rode in silence, counting off the minutes as best as they could.

At one point, King Rupert and Artemas fell into a quiet conversation. Ulric soon joined in the talk. Christopher listened to the discussion to drive away his boredom.

"Are we being followed, Ulric?" the king asked.

"I'm quite certain. Ever since we departed from the castle, I was aware of the stranger. I thought it best to proceed normally until he makes a move," Ulric said.

Artemas nodded. "He remains far enough behind us so as not to be too obvious."

"And to make a getaway should we pursue him."

"*Should* we go after him?" King Rupert inquired. "If he's going to pose a threat, I think we ought to. I won't have some nuisance of a spy jeopardizing our mission!"

"I don't think we have to worry," Ulric said. "My instincts tell me that we're not in any danger yet. Chasing after him will only delay us. Let him come after us if he must."

Ulric gently snapped the reins on his horse and moved out in front again as the conversation ended. Christopher's interest perked up and he felt the journey taking a turn for the better. He glanced over his shoulder but was unable to catch a glimpse of the spy. "They must have better eyesight than I do to be able to see in this gloom," he thought. Christopher asked Molly how she liked their adventure now that a genuine spy was tracking them. But all Molly did was lean back against her brother, fast asleep.

Near midnight the king decided that a short rest was in order. The travelers dismounted and soon Ulric had a small fire burning. All welcomed the warmth and light as they huddled about the snapping flames. A meal of dried meat, bread and water refreshed everyone, renewing their strength and spirit for the many miles ahead.

"How much farther tonight?" Molly asked, rubbing her eyes. "I don't suppose we'll find an inn along the way."

"Not in this barren wasteland," the king said. "A few hours more and then we'll make camp. How are you holding up, Molly?"

"Pretty good for my first adventure." But what Molly really wanted to say was how tired to the bone she felt, and how terribly she missed her parents and little Vergil. Sunrise couldn't arrive fast enough to please her.

Upon finishing their meal, Artemas smothered the fire and everyone packed up their things. They quickly mounted the horses and rode onward through the cold night air.

Another hour passed, then two, then three, but the dreary landscape seemed never-changing. The mountains to the left were still as bleak and uninviting as ever, and the darkness weighed upon them all. Only the stars had shifted their positions as they sank in the west one by one.

Though Christopher and Molly weren't aware of it, they had been slowly rising in elevation over the great plains in the last few hours. Ulric, quite familiar with the landscape, told the others to halt at one point while he rode on to scout the terrain ahead. The muffled footfalls of his steed in the shadows announced his return several minutes later.

"We have arrived sooner than I expected," he announced.

"We're at Malaban's fortress already?" Molly said hopefully. Despite the danger ahead, she wanted nothing more than to be warm and snug inside, no matter whose castle it might be.

Ulric laughed to himself. "You're quite anxious to end this journey, Molly. Though I hate to disappoint you, we are still a ways off from our destination. But we have made substantial progress." Ulric indicated for the group to follow. "Come with me and I will show you."

They rode their horses to the area which Ulric had scouted out. The children could see that they were now very high up overlooking a great expanse of land and dark rivers. "That is the Pinecrest Valley below. There used to be much trade and traveling through that valley by the people of Endora and other kingdoms," he said. "But that has stopped in recent times."

"Why?" Molly asked.

"Because at the end of the valley, Malaban awaits in his evil fortress. He keeps a watchful eye on all who dare to trespass," Ulric whispered. "Including us."

"I don't like the look of that land," Molly said. "It's very dreary and sinister."

"Hopefully the daylight will cheer it somewhat." Ulric pointed at a small object in the distance. "Do you see that hill just visible against the horizon?"

Christopher squinted to get a better look. "Just barely. What's so special about it?"

Ulric lowered his voice even further. "At the base of that hill awaits our sorcerer. Malaban's castle is built there, and we will have an unfriendly greeting party to welcome us if we are not careful."

Christopher sighed. "Thanks for telling us."

"It is good that you learn all the dangers ahead of you," he advised. "That way you can prepare. Now let's move on." Ulric urged his horse forward. "We'll travel a little ways down into the valley before making camp for the night. We can't risk a fire up here so open to everyone's view. As we descend, the small hills will shield us from Malaban's sight. At least for a short while."

Ulric led the others skillfully down the grassy slope. Though neither Christopher nor Molly was anxious to enter the valley, they knew that a few hours of sleep awaited them there, sleep they desperately needed to face the enemy.

They pitched their small tents on the east side of a grassy knoll to shield themselves from the wind. Molly and Christopher shared a tent, while the king and Artemas each pitched one of their own. Ulric preferred sleeping under the stars than inside a tent when the weather permitted, and would do so tonight.

He lit a fire before they retired for the night, and everyone ate another small meal while sitting bundled near the warm flames. Artemas gazed at the stars and King Rupert seemed lost in thought. Ulric walked about the campsite to inspect the area, but had nothing of interest to report. Christopher and Molly were simply content having a bite to eat and a place to sit.

With strength returning to her weary limbs, Molly felt up to posing a question to King Rupert. "What time will we continue traveling tomorrow? After lunch perhaps?"

"That would suit me splendidly," he said. Molly was delighted with the news. "However, such a long delay wouldn't help our mission. So I'm afraid we'll leave at the crack of dawn. With luck, we'll arrive sometime tomorrow night."

Molly wrinkled her lips into a sour frown. "At dawn! That hardly gives me time to close my eyes."

"You'll get a few hours rest. That should do."

Molly reconsidered. "I guess if your daughter has to put up with being a prisoner, I can live with only a few hours sleep. How old is your daughter anyway?"

King Rupert was slow to answer, for his thoughts were with Rosalind and the trials she might be suffering. But he vowed to find his daughter alive and well. "Rosalind is in her fourteenth year. But keep in mind that our year is somewhat longer than yours. She'll appear a bit older by your standards." He glanced at the magician. "Artemas, now that you are familiar with time in Molly's world, perhaps you can figure out how old Rosalind would be in her reckoning?"

Artemas scratched his head. "Seeing that I have no writing implements, my mind will have to do all the work. Let's see now," he mused, gazing into the heavens. "I would roughly estimate that Rosalind is close to eighteen years old according to Molly's calendar."

"Thank you, Artemas," Molly said. "Now if you all don't mind, I'm going to bed now. I wish to use every available minute to sleep." With that, Molly headed straight for her tent, climbed into her sleeping bag and promptly dozed off.

Exhaustion soon crept over the other travelers, and one by one they retired for the night. Ulric kept watch for a while next to the glowing embers of the dying fire. But even he could not hold back weariness indefinitely, and soon nodded off to sleep.

A thin streak of orange and red threaded its way across the horizon. Icy silence coated the plains like a deadly frost. Nothing moved. Not even a slight breeze rustled the brittle grass or the canvas tents. The horses stood in their silent sleep.

In an instant the stillness was ripped apart. Shouts and cries trumpeted in the dawn. A struggle ensued on the ground near the pile of cold gray embers. The travelers, warm inside their tents, were roused by a call for help.

"Awake! Awake! The spy has found us," Ulric shouted as he wrestled with the intruder.

King Rupert, Artemas, Christopher and Molly bolted from their tents and rushed to Ulric's aid. Though it was five against one, the stranger put up a fierce struggle trying to escape, but finally gave in, collapsing to the ground in exhaustion. The others stood round him, wiping the dirt and grass from their clothes, waiting for their spy to sit up. The man got to his knees as the sky grew lighter, plucking a clump of grass from his tangled hair. He coughed and rubbed his arms for warmth, then stood up, staring miserably at his stunned adversaries.

"Well what are you all gawking at?" Mr. Smithers said with a grunt.

"You!" Christopher said. "*You're* our spy?"

"What are you doing in my world?" King Rupert demanded to know. "Nobody invited you here."

Mr. Smithers rolled his eyes. "And nobody invited *you* into my world. But you were there anyway."

The king reconsidered. "Well—we're even on that point. But still—explain yourself!"

"Who is this man?" Ulric asked. "How do you know him?"

Molly took the liberty of explaining. "Mr. Smithers owns a diner in our world. We stopped there to wait for the timedoor to reopen. He obviously followed Christopher and me through it."

"Can you blame me?" Mr. Smithers asked. "Everyone just barges into my diner for breakfast, then scurries out in groups without paying the bill. Who wouldn't be suspicious? I never trusted you two since I laid eyes on you," he added, pointing a finger at King Rupert and Artemas. "When I saw the kids run out after you, I followed them to get to the bottom of things." Mr. Smithers looked about the barren landscape. "And it seems I did just that. Quite an invention, that—timedoor, did you call it?"

Now that all were convinced their spy wasn't really a spy, they sat down for breakfast, allowing Mr. Smithers to finish his tale. He said he sneaked up on the camp to look for food when Artemas tackled him to the ground. Mr. Smithers also wanted to know all about the timedoor, so Artemas kindly explained the mechanism to him. Molly gasped when Mr. Smithers admitted hiding behind the magician's coat tree after passing through the timedoor. "It was so cluttered all around with cloaks and scarves and boots, that I was able to hide behind it without being noticed. I saw you kids looking around just after I entered the room."

"Then I *did* hear somebody behind me!" Molly said. "After looking out into the hallway, I turned around expecting to see Artemas or King Rupert, but nobody was there. That's when the timedoor closed."

"Afterwards, I did my own spying around the castle," Mr.

Smithers continued. "When I learned the five of you were going to leave, I thought it best to follow. I figured I'd be safer chasing you than getting caught by some of your guards."

"My guards would have tossed you in prison if they'd caught you," the king said. "You would have been treated kindly until my return, but probably bored to tears."

When the talk died down after breakfast, King Rupert decided to allow Mr. Smithers to join them on the rescue. He was more than eager to accept and couldn't wait to get started. "Life back home is so dull. My diner is falling apart and hardly anyone ever stops by. I don't care if I ever return."

After the tents were packed and the group ready to move on, everyone wondered how Mr. Smithers was going to travel. He ran off into a patch of bush and tall grass and soon returned with a horse trotting contentedly behind him. "I borrowed him from one of your stables, King Rupert. Hope you don't mind."

"That makes little difference now. But I won't begrudge you a horse. In fact, I'm glad to have another member with the party," the king said. "The closer we get to the fortress, the more uneasy I become."

"Thank you," Mr. Smithers replied, flattered that King Rupert found him to be a worthy addition. "I am honored to assist you," he added with a slight bow, then immediately stood and snapped his fingers as if remembering something. "Oh, by the way, there's a question I've been meaning to ask you, King Rupert. Whatever happened to that other member of your group? Didn't he make it back through the timedoor?"

King Rupert and Artemas looked guiltily at each other, then the king shrugged his shoulders. "Only Artemas and I went through the timedoor into your world. I don't know who you're talking about. Well, let's go!" he said, ready to climb back on his horse.

Mr. Smithers scratched his head. "No, no, no! I'm sure there were *three* of you. Artemas and yourself, and that other fellow I followed to the caves. I assumed you all got separated." Everyone looked at the king who had one foot on the ground and the other lodged in a stirrup. "Don't you remember him? He looked kind of spooky. The one wearing the black cloak."

Christopher and Molly walked towards the king as he removed his foot from the stirrup. He looked at the children, red in the face, then glanced at Artemas for advice. "Who was that other person, King Rupert?" Christopher asked.

"Other person? Well I—I, um, uh, well . . . "

Molly looked up at Mr. Smithers. "Are you saying someone else besides King Rupert and Artemas entered our world through the timedoor?"

"That's exactly what I'm saying. But whoever he was, he didn't seem very pleased staying there. Many times I saw him beneath the bridge by the river, furiously tapping at the stone support as if looking for something." Mr. Smithers chuckled. "I thought he looked silly, but now I know better. He was probably trying to find that magic door, only it was closed."

"Enough idle talk!" the king said. "We have a mission to complete. So let's stop wasting time and get on with it!"

"But we want to know about this other person," Christopher insisted.

"Mr. Smithers has a wild imagination. He doesn't know what he's talking about," the king said, throwing a disdainful glance at the man. But no matter how often and loudly King Rupert ordered the others to follow him, nobody moved an inch.

"What are you trying to hide?" Christopher asked. Neither the king nor Artemas appeared eager to offer an explanation. They stood like two children who had been scolded by their parents.

Molly gently took hold of King Rupert's hand and softly spoke. "Please tell us, King Rupert. Tell us about that man in the black cloak."

King Rupert stood at a loss for words. All eyes were focused on him. He wiped the sweat from his brow and took several deep breaths. But not feeling any better and seeing no way of escaping the truth, the king plopped down onto the cold ground, holding his head and moaning. "I've been a bad king," he mumbled. "A very, very bad king. What a dreadful thing I've done." Then he went silent.

Several anxious minutes passed before the others could get the king to speak. The children were curious yet fearful about what he had to say. Finally, after a few kind words of support from Molly, King Rupert decided to tell everything, including even the tiniest detail.

"I always suspected you were hiding something," Christopher said. "But I could never figure out what."

King Rupert nodded. "I confess that I never told you the complete story. My castle *was* attacked by Malaban's troops, who also kidnapped my daughter Rosalind. And Artemas and I *did* flee through the timedoor to escape the sorcerer's wrath. That is all completely and honestly true as the air is cold," he said. "But there is something else. One little item I neglected to mention."

"Tell us," Molly whispered.

"When Artemas and I escaped through the timedoor, we entered your world in the early morning. A dense fog rolled on the ground. The two of us ran and hid behind some nearby bushes and waited." King Rupert combed his fingers through his hair. "We watched the bridge, and watched and waited till we saw what we had feared the most. A dark figure emerged from underneath the bridge and quickly searched the area. Not finding us, he headed off along the road by the river, thinking we had gone that way."

Christopher's jaw dropped. "Do you mean to say—?"

"Yes, Christopher," the king said. "It was the sorcerer. Malaban had followed us through the timedoor."

Molly couldn't believe her ears. "Malaban was in our world? In my very own neighborhood?"

"I'm afraid so, Molly," Artemas said, taking over for King Rupert who appeared too upset to talk anymore. "When King Rupert and I saw Malaban walk away, we rushed back under the bridge to the timedoor. But we were too late. So we ran down the road in the opposite direction, not wanting to run into Malaban. We took refuge in a deserted building in a field."

"Mrs. Halloway's barn!" Christopher shouted.

"We thought it best to hide out there until the timedoor re-opened. But then you children found us, and well, you know the rest of the story."

"Not all of it." Christopher looked directly at King Rupert. "Why did you lie about when the timedoor would reopen? Artemas calculated that it would open at sunrise."

"I can explain that," the king said. "After Artemas completed his work at the planetarium, he secretly informed me that the timedoor would open about an hour *before* sunrise. I instructed him to tell your father that it would open *at* sunrise."

"But why?"

"Because Artemas and I didn't want to return to Endora until the last possible moment," King Rupert explained. "If Malaban was watching nearby and saw us return through the timedoor, he would be certain to follow us. So I figured that if we waited till the very last moment, then the door would close before anyone else could go through. That's why I wanted to get rid of everybody at Mr. Smithers' diner. The less commotion, the better the chances my plan had to work." King Rupert looked around at Christopher, Molly and Mr. Smithers. "Well, I guess my timing was off a little. The three of you made it through. But apparently Malaban hasn't. My kingdom will be rid of him forever!" shouted King Rupert jubilantly. He frowned soon after when seeing that the children were less than enthusiastic with the news. "What's wrong?"

"What's *wrong*?" Christopher said. "Think about it. Malaban won't cause anymore trouble in your world, but imagine what he'll do while in ours!"

Molly shook her finger angrily at the king. "How could you pull a stunt like that? As soon as Malaban realizes he can't get back to his world, he'll start taking over ours. That sorcerer will prob-ably turn everyone into snakes and dragonflies and wiggle worms before the week is over!"

"I hadn't thought of that. I just wanted to get rid of the pest. I never meant to cause your world any trouble," the king said. "Dear me, but I've *really* fouled things up."

"And how!" Molly said.

"But just what are you going to do about it?" Christopher added.

The king looked at the children with shame in his eyes. What a horrible thing he had done, he thought. Staring at Christopher and Molly and seeing the worry etched on their faces, he couldn't help but think of his own daughter. How it pained King Rupert to imagine what hardships Princess Rosalind was enduring. He vowed not to let Malaban cause trouble for anyone else.

"Did you say that you watched the sorcerer?" the king asked Mr. Smithers.

"Yes, sir. After I saw him return to the bridge several times, I decided to follow him and see what he was up to." Mr. Smithers lowered his voice. "Malaban hid in an old cave about a half mile down the road near the river. I saw where he entered, but I never dared to go inside myself."

The king considered his options, then addressed his audience. "I have decided what to do. After we rescue Rosalind and return to my castle, we shall wait for the timedoor to reopen its last time. And since I got us into this mess, I guess I shall have to get us out. Therefore," he said in a booming voice, but paused a very long time afterwards, "I will return through the timedoor and confront Malaban myself. I shall drag that evil sorcerer back through the timedoor by his collar if I have to."

Everyone cheered at the good news. King Rupert tried to smile, but he now felt like he was carrying the world on his shoulders.

"Don't worry," Christopher said, sensing the king's uneasiness. "I will go with you. I'm not afraid."

"Me too!" Molly added. "If we can face Malaban's whole army to rescue Princess Rosalind, then dealing with Malaban alone should be a snap."

King Rupert shuddered. "Easier said than done, Molly. Though my heart tells me I'm a brave king for proposing to go after him, my mind insists that I'm a fool. Malaban will probably turn me into a sniveling field mouse and crush me underfoot before I even get a chance to speak!"

Though hardly the best sentiment to begin the remainder of their journey, it would have to do. Ulric led the way, though their travels that day proved uneventful. On occasion they stopped at a stream, usually frozen over, and broke through the top layer of ice to get at the refreshing water below. Mile by mile they continued north towards Malaban's fortress. The only thing that cheered them was the fact that Malaban wouldn't be there to greet them. But this proved to be a minor consolation after Ulric described the army of men and trolls and goblins that would be there instead.

Evening finally arrived, bringing with it a light snowfall. The change in weather cheered the children, but after an hour or two, the powdery flakes disappeared. The landscape was again a brown and barren wasteland. Molly seemed ready to give up altogether when Ulric halted the procession.

"Close enough. We'll make camp in that grove of trees over there," he whispered, pointing to a few dozen swaying pine trees. Their sweet scent refreshed the weary riders. "Malaban's fortress is about a mile due north. We'll sleep for a while, then leave a few hours before dawn. Get all the rest you can," Ulric strongly advised. "The path ahead is a dangerous one. And from this point on we travel by foot."

CHAPTER SIX

The Fortress Of Malaban

Christopher awoke several hours after midnight and peeked out of the opening in his tent. The stars glistened warmly in bunches, but the air bit with a stinging chill. He struggled to put on his coat and hood so as not to wake Molly, wrapped an extra blanket around his shoulders, then stepped outside. As tired as he had been a few short hours ago, all desire for sleep had now vanished. Christopher knew everyone else would be getting up in the next hour, so he decided to stay awake and enjoy the solitude.

He trudged over the dead grass to where the cold embers from last night's fire lay scattered. Christopher sat on a rock but immediately jumped up when hearing a twig snap. A dark figure emerged from the shadows. Christopher's heart pounded till he recognized the face in the gloom.

"Oh, it's you, Ulric. For a minute I thought we might have another spy to deal with."

"Starting today, *we* will be the spies," he said, setting down a pile of twigs and branches he had collected. "Breaking into a castle involves a bit of trickery."

"Oh, I've done that before," Christopher said in jest, though he was rather pleased that he and Molly had found King Rupert before the castle guards had found them.

"So you have," Ulric said with a grin. He built up a small pile of dried grass, leaves and wood shavings, then removed two small stones from his coat pocket. Ulric repeatedly struck one stone against the other, holding them close to the tinder. In a few moments, several hot sparks jumped from the stones and ignited the dry material. Ulric slowly added some small twigs, then a few larger ones, till a steady blaze burned. "I'll wake the others soon. I always like to get a fire going first," he said. "There's nothing worse than waking up with only the bitter darkness to greet you."

Christopher watched in fascination as the flames darted into the air. Quiet times like this were a pleasure, and the burden of the task ahead didn't weigh down so heavily. A part of him rather looked forward to the adventure. The thrill of a heroic rescue was something he had only dreamed about before, but now he was actually living it. If only his friends at school could see him now. Yet deep down inside, Christopher knew this wasn't a game. Images of the dangerous reality that lay ahead always lurked in the back of his mind.

"Ulric, do you think we'll rescue Princess Rosalind? There are only six of us against a whole army of soldiers. Those aren't very good odds."

Ulric agreed. "But we know our opposition from the start, so that is an advantage. They, on the other hand, do not know we are coming." The king's chief guard added more wood to the fire then stretched out his legs. "Once we get near the castle, we'll take matters one step at a time. We really don't know what to expect, so it's best to keep our options open."

Christopher found no fault with Ulric's logic and said nothing more. Both sat in silence and enjoyed the hypnotic crackle of the flames. An hour or so later, Ulric went around to each tent and wakened the others. Christopher heard the grumbling of the other members of the party as they crawled out of their tents. Then after a short breakfast under the cover of darkness, all were ready to go.

The tents were quickly folded and packed with all the other supplies. Everything not needed for the hike to Malaban's castle was hidden deep within the pine trees to await the group's return.

Even the horses had to be let go. Ulric explained that if a stray horse was spotted near the fortress, suspicions would be raised and a search party sent out. That's why it would be necessary to walk the final mile.

"There's a stream in the woods that is not frozen over," he said. "And plenty of grass for food and trees for protection. The horses will be better off than we are. If we're lucky, we will find them in this area when we return. I would hate walking all the way back to Endora."

But before anyone dared even to think that far ahead, they first had to travel north to rescue Princess Rosalind. So without further stalling, Ulric led the way across the dreary landscape, following along the woods to their right.

King Rupert feared that such a long hike over the cruel terrain would be too much for Molly, but was pleasantly surprised to see otherwise. During much of the walk she and Christopher gleefully discussed with Artemas the strange number of constellations in the sky.

"Daddy would be fascinated if he could see these stars," Molly said. "There are even more here than in our own night sky."

Artemas seemed doubtful. "You probably don't see as many stars back home because of all the dreadful light that blocks them from your view. I remember those monstrous metal light giants that stood guard over all your city streets. They emitted such an awful glare that I could hardly see a single star at times."

Christopher laughed at the magician. "Those were streetlights. Not giants."

"Well they're a nuisance to be sure."

"Our world isn't perfect," Mr. Smithers admitted. "But I'm happy to say that we don't have half-crazed sorcerers running around raising all sorts of havoc." Then he remembered that Malaban was hiding out in a cave not far from his own diner. "Well, *one* sorcerer anyway," he muttered, shrugging his shoulders. "What harm can *one* do?"

Before anyone could answer, Ulric rushed back to the group from his lead position and swiftly herded them into the edge of the woods. "Quiet," he whispered, signaling for everyone to squat down to keep hidden in the trees.

For the first time during the journey, Molly was genuinely frightened. She clutched Christopher's arm, waiting for whatever terrible thing was about to happen. Then she heard it, faint at first, but growing stronger—the pounding of footsteps. A hundred pairs of them, and possibly more. The rhythmic marching shook the ground. Brittle grass and twigs snapped and crunched as they were crushed beneath the weight of the approaching feet. Molly held her breath.

From behind a grassy hill emerged a hoard of hungry, dirty and grim-faced soldiers. They marched in twos and carried torches—men, trolls and goblins all mixed together. They traveled on a dirt road that came out from behind the hill and curved around, continuing along the woods farther north. Molly realized they were lucky to have had Ulric scouting ahead. If they had hiked on another minute longer, their group would have found the road just as the soldiers approached. All would certainly have been made instant captives. Instead of rescuing Princess Rosalind, they would have joined her in prison.

"Let them pass," Ulric softly said. "They won't see us hidden here in this darkness."

"I didn't realize we were so close to the fortress," King Rupert whispered.

"We're still a half mile away. But I wasn't expecting to come across a road at this point. It must be new. We'll follow it ourselves after the troops are out of sight. We'll save a good deal of time that way."

They took to the road in a short time and made swift progress. Ulric guessed that the road probably extended right to the castle gate. "We must be careful," he said. "Even though the hour is still early, there seems to be much activity near the castle. I wonder what's happening inside?"

"We'll find out soon enough," Christopher said, pointing. "Look."

There stood Malaban's fortress, looming in the distance like a huge squatting vulture. It was built out of black and gray slabs of stone, surrounded by a moat nearly sixty feet across. Guard towers shot up from each corner of the castle, and a stone parapet encircled the walkways high above the iron doors. The torchbearing soldiers they had encountered earlier were now marching across the drawbridge and disappeared inside.

"Surely we're not planning to march merrily across the drawbridge and go inside ourselves?" Mr. Smithers asked. "I see guards standing near the entrance."

"I'm not that brave *or* foolish to suggest such a plan," Ulric said. "Besides, the drawbridge is starting to close."

Mr. Smithers watched as the drawbridge was slowly raised with a groan by a pair of enormous black chains, then sealed shut with an echoing boom. "So much for that option," he said.

"This talk is all very well and good," the king interrupted, "but I suggest we get off the road at once. Spies might still be about, and dawn is not far off."

Ulric agreed and so they all slipped back into the woods and walked till they found a small clearing to rest. Molly sat down and leaned against a tree. "Now what?" she asked. "I'm glad we made it this far, but I haven't the slightest idea about how to get inside."

"I'm piecing together the beginnings of a plan," Ulric said. He invited the others to gather around to hear him out. "As we neared the castle, I started to recall a few details about it the last time I was in this area many years ago. If I remember correctly, there are a number of small doorways spread out around the base of the castle. They are used as escapeways for the people inside in case of an attack. Otherwise, they are most certainly never used."

"How will that help us?" Christopher asked.

"We simply find one of these doors and break inside," Ulric said casually. He saw the doubt registering on the boy's face. "Maybe I made it sound simpler than it really is. I suggest we stay just inside the woods and travel along the edge. Since these woods travel part way around the castle, we should be able to spot one of those escape doors with little difficulty."

"And then?" Molly asked.

"We'll cross that bridge when we get to it," Ulric replied. "Quickly now. We must be off before the light."

So they hiked along the edge of the woods with Malaban's castle always in view. Occasionally someone would stumble over a tree root or snap a large twig, causing everybody to stand still as statues and hold their breaths. But soon Artemas discovered what they were seeking.

"There!" He pointed to one section of the castle. "I can see one of those escape doors at the base of the building."

Ulric looked closely in the dispersing gloom. "I see it across the moat." Ulric stepped out of the woods and surveyed the surroundings, then signaled for the others to follow. "All clear now. We're on the east side of the castle. I can just make out the main entrance around the corner, so we still might be spotted from there if we're not careful. The drawbridge is up, so I don't expect a parade of troops just yet."

King Rupert led the others out of the woods, then the six of them ran across a small field between the trees and the castle under the last shadows of night. They soon came to a large bank that sloped down towards the moat. Ulric descended first, climbing over sharp rocks and tufts of dead grass and weeds, stopping now and then to catch his balance. King Rupert went next, trying to follow the same path as Ulric did, fearing he might stumble if he tried another. Christopher and Molly scurried down with ease, followed by Artemas and finally Mr. Smithers on the end.

When they made it to level ground, Molly looked up the bank and realized how steep it actually was. "We'll have to climb back up when we leave," she said, anticipating what a difficult task that would prove.

"Its steepness plays to our advantage," Ulric said. "We are quite hidden in its shadow for now, and are probably safer here than in the woods, at least until the sun rises."

The ground between the bottom of the bank and the edge of the moat extended about twenty feet. The moat itself stretched on for sixty feet. Across the water loomed the sheer east wall of the castle. Directly across at the base of it was a small iron door with a tiny barred window, locked from the inside. A narrow rocky shore led up to the door. Off to its left was a raft, secured with a rope tied to a metal ring cemented into the castle wall. Mr. Smithers spotted it first.

"Look!" he shouted, causing Ulric to ask him to lower his voice unless he wanted a visit from an angry troll. "Look," he repeated in a whisper. "If my eyes aren't playing tricks, I see a raft tied up on the left side of the door."

Artemas confirmed the discovery. "There is a raft, no doubt for the use of someone fleeing the castle."

"Just one problem," Ulric said. "The raft is on the wrong side of the moat to do us any good. Unless you care to swim across the freezing water and row it back."

"No thanks. I'd rather build a boat than get that one."

"That's just what we'll have to do unless we think of something soon," King Rupert said. "Our cover of darkness won't last forever."

The king was clearly frustrated at the halt in their progress, especially being so close to his daughter. The old man paced along the shore, then found a rotting log half buried in the dirt and sat down on it to think. Molly and Christopher sat beside him. King Rupert looked so glum that he reminded the children of the time they discovered him in Mrs. Halloway's barn.

"Don't give up hope yet," Molly said. "We've made it this far, haven't we?"

Christopher agreed. "You can't solve every problem in an instant. Remember all the trouble we went through just to find out when the timedoor would reopen?"

"I'm not giving up," the king sighed. "I'm just disappointed that we can't move any faster. Rosalind is locked away in this horrible place, and here I am sitting idly by on a log and not doing a bit of good. Curses on that Malaban! I'll give him a piece of my mind the next time I see him!" King Rupert's melancholy quickly transformed into a fiery anger, getting him back into the spirit of the rescue. He stood and waved his fist at the castle. "We're not defeated yet!" he shouted across the water.

"Feeling better?" Molly asked.

"I'm feeling angry!" the king said. "I'll get into that castle somehow, even if I have to rip this log out of the ground and paddle it across the water myself!"

Though most were amused with the king's rantings, Ulric saw the commonsense of it all. He laughed as he walked over to King Rupert and the children. "If only you boiled over like this more often. You might solve your matters of state much more quickly."

King Rupert squinted his eyes in puzzlement. "Don't speak in riddles, Ulric. What are you saying?"

"I'm saying we have found a way to get across the moat. Though *you* may not care to paddle across the icy water on a log, one of us can."

"A brilliant idea!" Artemas agreed. "So simple a solution that one of us should have thought of it sooner."

King Rupert thought so as well and urged everyone to grab a stone to help dig away at the dirt packed around the log. The task proved to be tiring and tedious, but after several minutes of furious digging and dirtying of fingernails, they freed the log and rolled it into the water.

The next step was to choose someone to sit on the log and paddle across the moat, untie the raft and row it back. The arguments boiled down to finding someone light enough so the log wouldn't submerge completely, as well as agile enough not to fall off. Though each insisted everyone else was more qualified for the task, Christopher volunteered in the end, if only to cease the bickering. A part of him thought it would be fun to paddle across a moat on a log since he would probably never have such an opportunity again.

Christopher removed his boots and socks, rolled up his pant legs and stepped into the moat. The freezing water chilled his toes and gave him goosebumps. He sat on the log as quickly and carefully as he could, then lifted his feet out of the water. "Better get this over with as fast as I can," he said to himself, plunging his feet back into the icy current and paddling off.

Sixty feet seemed like a mile. Christopher balanced himself extremely well, and after getting the log to sail along smoothly, he would lift his feet from the water till it stopped, then paddle some more. He didn't know which felt worse, the cold water or the winter air, but tried not to think much about either. He'd occasionally glance over his shoulder to see the shadowy figures of his friends standing on shore. They seemed so far away in the pale light.

The log stopped with a jolt when hitting the shallow end on the other side. Christopher jumped off and scurried out of the water. He found the raft by the iron door and untied a stubborn knot in the rope, freeing their prize. But before he left, Christopher tried to open the door out of curiosity. It was securely locked and he had no idea how they would ever open it.

A brief look up at the sky told him that dawn was about to break, so he dragged the raft into the moat and climbed aboard. A small oar was attached which Christopher used to paddle across, happy not having to stick his feet into the water again. He wondered if any strange monster lurked at the bottom of the moat, thankful he hadn't considered that possibility on the way over.

Ulric and Mr. Smithers pulled the raft to shore when Christopher arrived. The boy ignored them and ran over to Molly, who handed him his dry socks and boots. Christopher put them on then walked about the shore to warm up his feet. "I wouldn't want to do that again," he said to his sister. "Not for all the money in the world!"

King Rupert stepped onto the raft and stood bravely in front, his hands on his hips, facing the castle with a challenging gaze. After the others climbed aboard, Ulric placed the oar in the water and carried them swiftly across. He and Mr. Smithers dragged the raft back up the rocky shore and retied it as before in order not to raise suspicions should a guard happen to spot it later.

"Now to open the door," Ulric said, producing a small dagger from under his coat. "I'll try to pry the lock since there's no way to break down the door."

Ulric placed the tip of the dagger into the keyhole and worked the blade for several minutes. No success.

"Let me try," Mr. Smithers said.

"Be my guest." Ulric handed him the knife and Mr. Smithers went to work. But no shouts of joy followed, for his attempt failed as well.

"We'll be sitting ducks if you don't hurry!" Christopher said. "I can see the horizon getting lighter by the minute. The sun will rise soon."

If the approaching light wasn't enough of a problem, another one cropped up just as fast. A rumble of wood and metal echoed along the castle wall. Everyone looked left, and to their horror saw that the drawbridge was slowly descending.

"Gracious!" cried King Rupert. "We're doomed! Whoever crosses that bridge now is sure to see us. We *are* sitting geese!"

"Sitting *ducks!*" Christopher said.

Artemas rushed to the door. "Don't give up yet!" he said, indicating for Ulric and Mr. Smithers to step aside. The magician placed one hand firmly below the door handle and the other on the stone wall adjacent to it. "If muscle can't get us inside, maybe magic will." Artemas closed his eyes in deep concentration. His face tightened as if in pain. He appeared as still as stone for what seemed like an eternity. Molly almost called out to him, but Christopher stopped her.

The rumbling and groaning of the lowering drawbridge grew

louder and louder. At the same instant a ray of sunlight shot over the horizon, then another and another, and soon the rescuers were bathed in the morning light. All feared for their lives when a loud snap of metal cracked the air. Artemas fell backwards.

The children rushed to him. "Are you all right, Artemas?" Molly asked. She and Christopher helped him to his feet.

"I'll be fine. The door is unlocked! Everyone inside before it's too late!"

King Rupert opened the door with ease. He madly waved the others inside and followed them in last, slamming the door behind him. At the same instant the drawbridge landed and a double line of goblin troops marched out over the moat. The sun rose too and lit the castle walls with its morning brilliance. But the group from Endora was safe inside as the first light of the sun streamed in through the barred window.

The room smelled damp and musty. Flimsy strands of ancient cobwebs were strung everywhere. Since there wasn't a torch fastened to the wall, the group had to wait for the full daylight to reveal their surroundings. All they could determine right now was that the stone room was small and quite overcrowded with six people inside. A little more light revealed a staircase leading up to the ground level. From the dirty look of things, it appeared that nobody had been down here in quite a few years.

Artemas sat on the floor to rest, propping his back against the wall. Opening the door with a blast of magic had worn him out.

"Are you feeling better?" Molly asked. "I didn't realize magic was so dangerous."

"My powers feel a bit rusty. Ever since I visited your world, my magic requires more and more effort. Why, it took me forever to grow that grapevine in your living room."

Molly remembered and hoped that Artemas would feel better

soon. Everyone had their off days and she concluded that magicians could have them too.

Ulric, in the meantime, examined every corner of the tiny chamber. "Time to find out where this staircase leads." He bounded up the dozen or so steps and the darkness deepened around him.

"What do you see?" King Rupert whispered from below. He kept a watch through the barred window, observing the drawbridge as best he could.

Ulric soon returned. "The stairs lead to a small passage about ten feet long. It's black as night up there. There's a door at the end of the passage, so I peered through the keyhole."

"What'd you see?" Mr. Smithers asked.

"The door opens into the main floor of the castle. But the area looked deserted. Even though it's early morning, I had expected to see a guard at least."

"Well there *are* guards," the king said, pulling back from the window. "I see them now. About a half dozen trolls and goblins are patrolling the area. Monstrous looking beasts. We made it inside in the nick of time. What do you suggest now, Ulric?"

"We should go upstairs and split into two groups and begin our search for Princess Rosalind. I don't know why there aren't any guards in the area outside the door, but let's use that to our advantage while we can."

"Agreed," King Rupert said. "Lead on."

They ascended the staircase in single file, disappearing from each other's sight in the choking darkness. As his eyes adjusted, Christopher detected the outline of a doorway at the end of the passage. Ulric made a final check through the keyhole, and judging the way still clear, opened the door.

They walked into a vast chamber, bare except for several torches fixed to the walls. This was a point where three wide corridors met, one branching off to the left, one to the right, and a third one going straight ahead. Ulric reasoned that the passage to the left would lead back to the main entrance of the castle, so he advised against going that way. King Rupert gave the final instructions.

"We will search this level of the castle to begin with, then return to our hiding place to determine where we stand," he said.

"And if anyone is caught," Ulric added, "make no mention of the others. The less our enemy knows, the better our chance to defeat him."

In the end, King Rupert, Ulric and Molly searched the hallway extending straight ahead. Christopher, Artemas and Mr. Smithers took the passage to the right. Neither group had any idea where they were going or what to expect—or if they would ever return.

CHAPTER SEVEN

Apples, Maps and Magic

Christopher, Artemas and Mr. Smithers moved warily along the passageway. Several wooden doors lined each side of the corridor, but opening them led to no important discoveries. Smaller hallways branched off from the main passage now and then, but Artemas decided that it would be best to ignore them for now. "We'll only get lost if we explore every little twist and turn in this wretched place."

Behind one door Christopher discovered a spacious dining hall crammed full of wooden tables and benches. "I'll bet three hundred people could fit in here," he said in amazement. "I'm just glad we didn't barge in during breakfast. I don't think we'd have been invited in for eggs and toast."

"Unlikely," Mr. Smithers said, at the same time wondering what exactly trolls and goblins *did* eat for breakfast. "If only there was a kitchen to go along with this dining hall. I'd be curious to compare it to the kitchen in my own diner."

"We're here to rescue Princess Rosalind," Artemas reminded him sternly. "We don't have time to browse."

"I know," he replied while carefully opening another door. "I'm merely curious." But before Artemas could respond, Mr. Smithers threw up his arms like a referee signaling a touchdown. "Bingo! My wish is granted." Christopher and Artemas ran over, warning him to lower his voice. But Mr. Smithers ignored them and rushed inside the room. He had found his kitchen after all.

The room connected to the dining hall and was likewise deserted, allowing Mr. Smithers an excuse to look about like a child through a toy store. A large fireplace was against one wall. Next to it was a stone oven built into the wall for baking. Wooden shelves and cupboards lined the room, and a large butcher's block stood in the center. In one corner was a filled water barrel, and a stale loaf of bread lay on one of the counters. What appealed to the group most were the sacks of apples and potatoes lined up against a wall. Their sweet fragrance filled the room.

"What luck!" Mr. Smithers plucked an apple from one of the bags. "What better place for breakfast than right here. I'm starving. If one of you two could find some spices, a bit of pepper and parsley perhaps, I think I could throw a stew together. And bread and butter. Look for that too."

Mr. Smithers bit into the apple, then searched through the cupboards looking for dishes and utensils to prepare his meal. Christopher and Artemas watched in disbelief.

"What's the matter with you?" Artemas said. "A guard could walk in here any minute. We have to move on!"

He and Christopher ushered Mr. Smithers out of the room in spite of his protest, and continued down the passageway. Though Mr. Smithers eventually admitted his foolishness in delaying their search, he still insisted that a hot potato stew would have been well worth the risk.

After several more minutes of fruitless inspection, Christopher began to wonder if they should turn around and go back and wait for the others. "All we're finding is a lot of empty rooms. Where is everybody? What kind of castle is this?"

Artemas scratched his head. "I'm not sure, Christopher. It is strange not to find at least some guards milling about. But we should go on a short while more."

So the monotonous search continued, and soon the trio came to an opening in the passage. The area branched off into three more corridors, similar to the area where they began their search. Artemas decided that the group would split up to cover more ground in less time.

"I'll go straight ahead. Christopher, you search the right passage. Mr. Smithers, you go left. And remember, stay on this level."

The group split up. Christopher was uneasy being on his own at first, wondering whether some large troll or hideous goblin might pop out of one of the doors at any instant. He hoped he could outrun such a creature. But he soon forgot his fears when he stumbled upon a small room at the end of his corridor. Bright sunlight streamed in through a window, making his surroundings warm and pleasant. It was a map room. Large colorful maps were fastened to every wall, and a whole shelf along one side contained scores of rolled up maps and charts of every place imaginable in this strange world.

Christopher first examined the largest map on the wall, and to his delight found that it was the only place he was familiar with. Before his eyes, colored in pale brown, was the kingdom of Endora. The boy slowly traced his finger along the path he had taken across the plains, stopping when it landed upon Malaban's castle in the Pinecrest Valley.

As interesting as the map was, Christopher realized the information didn't do him any good in locating Princess Rosalind. So he turned to leave when his eye caught sight of a small map on the wall near the exit. Christopher looked closer and discovered that it appeared to be a diagram of the castle. A small black dot on the map marked the very room in which he stood.

"This is just what we need!" But before Christopher could examine it further, he heard Artemas frantically calling from a distance. He dashed out of the map room to find him.

Christopher nearly collided with Mr. Smithers, who was also racing to find Artemas. They headed down the passage the magician had taken, finally discovering him inside a tiny room. He was hunched over a table cluttered with jars and vials filled with colorful powders and potions. The room resembled the magician's own chamber in King Rupert's castle.

"What's the matter?" Christopher asked, very much out of breath. "We heard you calling and thought you were in trouble."

Artemas looked up at his shaken companions. "I'm terribly sorry for my outburst, but when I found this room I couldn't contain my joy. Look around! This is a magician's paradise!"

Mr. Smithers smirked. "What's so special about this room? Everything's such a mess. Dust everywhere."

"This looks like your own chamber," Christopher said.

"Exactly. I believe this is Malaban's chamber where he practiced his sorcery. What a fortunate discovery. My own chamber pales compared to this!"

Artemas searched through every nook and corner of the room, making discoveries that excited him but meant little to Christopher and Mr. Smithers. The room contained five tables altogether, each very cluttered, and a fireplace with a mound of cold ashes and charred logs inside. Yellowed scrolls and dog-eared books were piled everywhere, and a row of hideous looking animal skulls lined a shelf near a window covered by dusty drapes. Pale morning light seeped in through holes in the material. There were also three tiny storage alcoves built into one wall, each covered by a thick red curtain. Artemas read through one of the scrolls, forgetting that his companions were watching and waiting in silence.

Mr. Smithers could tolerate it no longer. "Artemas! We're here to rescue a princess. *We don't have time to browse*! At least that's what you told *me* when I found my kitchen." Artemas glanced up with a raised eyebrow. "Now if you intend to quit our mission to stay here and dabble with magic potions, then I shall go back to my kitchen and make a potato stew!"

Christopher flinched, surprised that Mr. Smithers had addressed the magician so forcefully. But Artemas took the point well and set down the scroll.

"You're quite right, Mr. Smithers. We'll move on at once," was all he said, but not before gathering a few glass vials of colorful liquids and putting them in a sack he found lying on the floor. He handed it to Christopher. "These are some magic potions that might come in handy. Hold on to them for me. I forgot to pack some of my own back at the castle."

Christopher took the sack and tied it to his belt, then told the others about the map room as they headed for the door. Artemas stopped cold, placing his ear to the door and signaling for the others to be quiet.

"I hear something," he whispered. "Guards! Two of them. Trolls, I believe." Artemas turned to his friends. "And they're coming this way."

Since the sorcerer's room was so small and there wasn't a second exit, they had no choice but to hide inside one of the alcoves. They chose the one farthest from the door, closed the curtain, and waited anxiously in the darkness. What Artemas feared most happened next. The guards entered the chamber.

The large troll guards stood nearly seven feet tall, and neither were very happy having to patrol the castle so early in the morning. They had dark leathery skin and wore uniforms. One punched his partner in the arm, speaking in a low gruff voice.

"I told you nobody was in here, Nagg! Why don't you ever listen to me? You have rocks for brains!" the troll complained.

Nagg growled, exposing his sharp yellow teeth. "I know I heard voices!" He began to look around the room. "A shout came from down this passageway."

"You're hearing things, Nagg, you old troll!"

"Don't call me an old troll, Bolo, or I'll toss you out the nearest window!" Nagg examined a few of Malaban's scrolls.

"What are you doing, Nagg? Let's move on!"

"This is Malaban's room, you fool. I've never been in here before. Now that he's gone, what better time for a look?" Nagg said.

Bolo was angry with his partner, letting a stream of hot breath hiss through his teeth. "Who cares about sorcerer's tricks? We have to finish our patrol and get back to the meeting before Captain Urgot finds out we've been snooping."

"Curses on Captain Urgot and all the other men!" Nagg sputtered. "Ever since Malaban disappeared, they've taken over the castle. Do you ever see men on patrol duty? Do you see men marching in the cold outdoors? Never! It's all us trolls and goblins that get most of the dirty work. The meeting going on right now is just a waste of time. It's all for show. I'll bet you ten roasted squirrels that no troll or goblin will get picked as the new leader!"

"So what!" Bolo said. "There's nothing we can do about it. If you're so dead set against this place, why don't you run away?"

"I just might!" Nagg said, pointing a crooked finger at Bolo. But the sight of the curtained alcoves caught his fancy, so he dropped the argument for the moment. "Look at them over there. What do you suppose Malaban hides inside those?"

Bolo was just as intrigued as Nagg, scratching his chin in wonder. "I suppose a quick search wouldn't take too much time. Maybe there's a barrel of dried mudfish behind one. I could go for a snack right about now!"

"Now you're talking!" Nagg said, smacking his lips. He marched over to the alcove closest to the door and separated the curtains. "Nothing but sorcerer's junk!"

Bolo did the same to the middle alcove. "Even less behind this one. Why couldn't Malaban store something good in his chamber, like pickled frog livers? What I'd give for a bowl of those right now."

"You're making me hungry!" Nagg said. "I'll check inside the last one.

Christopher, Artemas and Mr. Smithers heard every word the trolls said. Their hearts pounded and their limbs trembled, knowing it was only a matter of time till they were caught. They braced themselves, ready to rush at the trolls as soon as the curtain was parted.

Nagg trudged over to the last alcove and placed his hands upon the curtain. He was about to swish it open when a bloodcurdling shout from the corridor sent both trolls into a panic. "It's Captain Urgot!" Bolo squealed in terror. "I told you we shouldn't waste time!"

"Let's get into the hallway before he catches us in here!" Nagg cried, sailing past his partner to reach the door first. In the next instant the trolls were gone, the room silent. The trio hiding inside the last curtained alcove breathed a collective sigh of relief.

Artemas poked his head out of the chamber door several minutes later. He didn't see or hear any sign of the troll guards, so he quickly led Christopher and Mr. Smithers back down the corridor to the point where they had earlier split up.

"Now what?" Mr. Smithers asked, craning his neck each way for signs of the trolls. "We can't stand here forever. Those creatures might return at any moment."

"Forget about them," Christopher said. "I have something important to tell you." With all the excitement, he hadn't finished telling them about his discovery. "I've found a map room, with maps of every place in this world!"

"All well and good," Mr. Smithers said. "But how's that going to help us find the princess?"

Christopher placed his hands on his hips. "There's also a map of this castle detailing every chamber. If we study it carefully—"

"—then we'll be able to locate the prisons! Good job," Mr. Smithers said.

"Show us this room right away," Artemas said. "That will be a safer place than standing in this hall waiting for some brute of a troll to come lumbering along."

Christopher quickly guided Artemas and Mr. Smithers through the passageway he had explored earlier and took them into the map room. Since narrowly escaping the trolls and now finding a map of the castle, all were filled with a new sense of hope and determination. Their chances of rescuing Princess Rosalind now seemed better than ever.

CHAPTER EIGHT

Above the Great Meeting Hall

Christopher closed the door to the map room. "We'll be safe in here." Artemas and Mr. Smithers looked in amazement at all the maps. "Didn't I tell you there were lots? Hundreds, I'd say."

"This is a much nicer room than the others," Mr. Smithers remarked. "Except for my kitchen."

"Oh, enough with your kitchen," Artemas said, then turned to Christopher. "Now where is that map of the castle you told us about?"

"Right there." Christopher pointed to the wall map near the door, and soon all were scrutinizing the diagram.

"Looks like a rat's maze to me," Mr. Smithers said.

"That's because you don't know how to read a map." Artemas let his eyes wander over the paper. "Hmmm . . . According to this, we are standing *here*." He pointed to a spot on the map. "There's the sorcerer's chamber we were just in. And there, Mr. Smithers, is your kitchen."

"But where are the prisons?" Christopher anxiously inquired. "There are so many chambers in this castle."

"Too many," Artemas agreed. "Ah ha! Here they are. On the level below us. But in order to reach them, we must go all the way to the other side of the castle. If I'm not mistaken—" he said, but then Artemas suddenly stopped to think out his strategy in silence.

"Is there a problem?" Christopher asked, studying the jumble of chambers.

"No, not a problem, but perhaps an advantage. Look here," Artemas pointed out. "These spaces are the prisons below, and over here is the passage that King Rupert and the others followed. Eventually they'll pass by this door right here and open it."

Mr. Smithers nosed up to the diagram. "What's so special about that door?"

"This particular door leads down to the prison cells. Maybe they'll be daring and explore below."

Mr. Smithers shook his head. "I don't think so. If you remember, each group was supposed to stay on this level of the castle."

"I recall," Artemas said. "But since this particular door opens up to a staircase and *not* a room, the king may get curious and check it out. If not, we'll tell the others about it when we return to our hiding spot. Then we'll *all* go to the prisons."

Christopher had hoped Artemas would say that. Why should King Rupert, Molly and Ulric have all the fun rescuing Princess Rosalind? He wanted to be in on the action too. "Let's go back now," Christopher said. "The sooner we leave, the sooner we can begin the rescue."

"We'll leave shortly. But there's something else I've discovered. Look at this," Artemas said.

Christopher and Mr. Smithers studied the map again but looked puzzled. "What's the big deal?" Mr. Smithers said. "You're pointing to another chamber. They all look alike. What's so special about *that* one?"

"That chamber looks like an enormous meeting hall, Mr. Smithers. If I remember correctly, those two troll guards had mentioned some sort of meeting was in progress."

"*That* explains where everyone is!" Christopher now understood what Artemas had in mind. "You want us to spy on their meeting."

"Can you think of a better way to find out what is going on in this miserable place?"

"Or a better way to get us all captured," Mr. Smithers said. "It'll be impossible to spy on hundreds of enemy soldiers without being spotted."

"Oh, have a little faith, sir. We've made it this far, haven't we?" The magician quickly filled them in on the details of his plan. "The meeting hall is on the main level, and I don't think there is a way we can sneak in. A dozen guards would nab us on the spot."

"My point exactly. So how are we to spy?" Mr. Smithers inquired.

Artemas referred to the map again. "Notice here along the top of the meeting hall. A narrow balcony encircles the entire chamber. The stairway leading up to the balcony is at the end of the passageway we're in right now. We can scramble up there in the blink of an eye. This is too important an opportunity to pass up."

"I think it's worth the risk," Christopher agreed. "Now that Malaban is gone, we should find out what his troops are up to. Maybe they're planning another invasion of Endora to rescue him."

"Good point," Mr. Smithers said. "All right. I'm willing to go along too. But I'm warning you, if I see some goblin or troll look up at us, I'm running out of there as fast as a pig to a mudhole! The last thing I want is to be a guest in their prison."

Satisfied that the passageway was clear, the trio left the map room and hurried along to the very last door on their right. Christopher opened it, revealing a dimly lit spiral staircase. Artemas entered first and the others followed.

They ascended the stone steps one by one. Christopher attempted to count them but gave up after forty-two. His legs began to ache by then, and he didn't care anymore about how many steps there were so long as they came to an end.

"How high up is this balcony?" Mr. Smithers panted.

"Patience," Artemas advised. "Look on the bright side. Chances are nobody will want to follow us."

"They won't have to. We'll probably collapse and die before we reach the top."

Despite the anguish of the steep climb, they eventually conquered the very last step. "At last!" Christopher said, plopping down on the floor. "Meeting or no meeting, I'm resting here for a moment." The vote was unanimous, so they all rested for a brief spell, catching their breath and allowing the pain to ease out of their tired limbs.

They sat in near total darkness except for a patch of light that slipped out beneath a doorway a few feet off. Artemas managed to stand and explore the area, only to find that they were in a very tiny passage with hardly enough room for a half dozen people.

"The balcony is behind this door," Artemas whispered. "I can hear the rumble of voices below. It must be an important meeting from the numbers I estimate."

"How many do you think are down there?"

"I would guess hundreds, Christopher. So when we go through the door we can only open it the slightest bit. Just enough for us to squeeze through on our hands and knees. If someone happens to glance up, we're finished." Artemas paused to let his warning sink in. "After we're out and I close the door, we must crawl along and keep our heads down. Let me have a quick look before we begin."

Artemas went to the door. Christopher sat paralyzed as he gently turned the knob and opened the door only wide enough to let a slit of light peek through. The rumble of voices in the meeting hall grew uncomfortably distinct. They were harsh and boisterous and apparently on the verge of exploding. Artemas closed the door.

"What did you see?" Mr. Smithers asked like an eager child. "What's happening down there?"

"I saw hundreds of angry faces. Men, trolls and goblins. They were everywhere! I couldn't hear what they were arguing about, but I'm sure it concerns Malaban's disappearance."

"Is there cover for us out there?" Christopher asked.

"The balcony railing is nearly three feet high. It is wooden, very old and dry with many splits in it. So we should be able to clearly see and hear what's happening. *Just keep down*! Are you ready?"

"Yes," Christopher said confidently, though Mr. Smithers just nodded his head.

"Then let us begin," the magician said in a solemn voice, as if they were about to meet their doom.

Artemas opened the door wide enough to crawl through. The angry voices below grew louder and louder as the three spies made their way onto the balcony. Christopher followed Artemas and Mr. Smithers was last, closing the door behind him. Then after pausing a moment, satisfied that none of them had been spotted, each found a place to watch the proceedings below, though cramped and uncomfortable all the while.

The great meeting room was ablaze with torches fastened to every wall and pillar and archway. Large wooden tables were set up everywhere, crowded with throngs of noisy men at some, trolls at others and goblins at all the rest. Mugs of warm ale cluttered the tabletops, and all drank as steadily as they argued. A wooden platform with a table on it was built along the center of the back wall. Seated at that table were the higher ranking officers in Malaban's army. Most were men, though a few trolls and a goblin or two were there as well. All in all, the vast chamber was hot and noisy and smelling of ale. Shadows from the flaming torches danced wildly on the walls, keeping time with the furious waving of fists of the raucous soldiers.

"Attention!" a man shouted from the platform. He stood tall with iron gray hair, dark eyes and a pointed jaw. A grim expression was painted on his face. He slammed his fist on the table, shaking it violently. "I said I want your attention! We've been arguing all night and now it is daylight. I demand a vote at once! It is useless to carry on like this."

A voice shot up from the crowd. "Easy for you to say, Belthasar!" a goblin exclaimed. He was short and plump with bulging eyes and yellowish skin. Several of his wide flat teeth were missing. "You're Malaban's chief guard, and most of the soldiers here are men. It's plain to see that *you'll* be voted to lead us. That's unfair! I say we should have three leaders—a goblin, a troll and a man!"

An eruption of shouting and pounding mugs shook the chamber. The trolls and goblins hooted their support for the idea. The men, especially Belthasar, were hardly enthused. Some tried to hide their fright behind stony faces.

Belthasar tried to calm the raging mob. "Since I was Malaban's chief guard, I am the best choice for your leader! I am the greatest among you! Why are you against me?"

Such arrogant talk proved to be more than the others could stand. Even the few trolls and goblins on the platform started to join in the chorus of protests. Every troll and goblin in the chamber jumped out of their seats and rushed to gather around the main table, demanding to be treated fairly. Their chanting was so loud that Christopher blocked his ears to keep them from hurting.

Belthasar was flustered. Sweat beaded up on his brow. He whispered to one of his nearby aides. "What can I do? They are on the verge of rioting. Curses on Malaban for bringing mountain creatures into this castle!"

The fearful aide quivered. "You—you haven't much choice, Belthasar," he said over the din. "Think of something to appease them quickly, or you won't be alive to get a second chance. Nor will I!"

Belthasar considered the warning as the shouting escalated and the trolls and goblins closed in around him with anger in their fiery eyes and hot breath. He resigned himself to the fact that he could never be solely in charge of the castle under these circumstances. So gathering all of his frazzled nerves and putting aside his pride, Belthasar called once again for silence. "I have an announcement!" he bellowed out, though he had to repeat this five or six times before the boiling mob settled down.

"What do you want, Belthasar?" a scowling troll shouted back, his red eyes filled with hate. "You better have something new to say because we've had it with your speeches!" The trolls and goblins raged again with delight, stomping their feet and shaking the room like an earthquake.

"Silence!" Belthasar's heart pounded till the room quieted, then he paused for what seemed like an eternity before making his announcement. "I have decided to appoint Arga the troll and Crull the goblin as chief guards over their own armies." Belthasar pointed to the troll and goblin sitting at the main table behind him. "Now there will be *three* leaders in the castle, though I will remain as a general overseer of the kingdom since I was Malaban's second in command. Are there any objections to *this* plan?" his said. Belthasar waited fearfully for a reply, certain that his offer would be rejected.

Arga and Crull stood to face each other, and after whispering between themselves for a few moments, they nodded their heads slightly.

"I accept your offer on behalf of the trolls," Arga said.

"I do the same for the goblins," Crull added.

At once the chamber of soldiers erupted in cheers and celebration. Belthasar sat back in his chair and breathed a sigh of relief. He had escaped disaster. After the crowd finally calmed down, Belthasar stood to again address the troops. "Now that Arga will command the trolls and Crull will be in charge of the goblins, I hope we will all be able to work together. As you know, we have a monumental task before us." Belthasar paused, enjoying the curious looks on everyone in the chamber. "Yes indeed. Now that we are united, I will finally reveal to you the details of my Great Plan!"

There were again shouts and cheers of approval from the crowd, for most had an inkling of what Belthasar's Great Plan involved. The soldiers hurried back to their seats, waiting impatiently for the exciting news. Christopher, Artemas and Mr. Smithers, glued to their places high up in the balcony, were equally curious as to what Belthasar had in mind, certain it would be evil to the core.

But before Belthasar could utter a word about his Great Plan, a small band of guards burst into the room, their leader rushing up to speak with Belthasar. "We have a gift for you!" he shouted, signaling for his soldiers to step forward.

They did so, escorting four individuals right up to the platform where Belthasar and his officers could inspect them. "And who have we here?" he demanded.

"Prisoners!" the guard shouted. "Four intruders who were not clever enough to escape under my watch."

The men, trolls and goblins jeered and hissed at the four cowering figures. Christopher gasped when he saw them and glanced at Artemas, his eyes ablaze in fear. The boy could not believe what he saw below.

CHAPTER NINE

A Fortunate Find

When Molly, King Rupert and Ulric had left earlier to explore another passageway, they were amazed that the castle appeared deserted. Ulric directed the search as Molly and the king followed, whispering to each other along the way.

"It's so quiet that it's spooky," Molly said. "I feel that a guard might burst out of a nearby room at any moment and capture us."

"Don't say such things!" King Rupert warned. "Bad enough that Rosalind was kidnapped. If we were apprehended, our mission would be a dismal failure. I could never forgive myself."

"Finally!" Ulric said, interrupting their conversation as he turned a corner in the passageway. Along both sides of the corridor was a series of closed doors. "At last we have something to search. Carefully listen at each door before opening it. If you hear any sound within, get away quickly."

So their search officially began. Molly was hesitant to open any door at first, fearing that something awful might be waiting for her on the other side. But after pressing her ear to four or five doors only to hear dead silence, she grew less and less afraid to peek inside.

King Rupert and Ulric discovered nothing interesting during their investigations either. "The whole place is empty!" the king said in wonder. "What kind of a castle is this? Either everyone is still asleep, or they're hiding somewhere, waiting to ambush us." Ulric agreed that the atmosphere inside was highly unusual, but urged everyone to continue with their search.

Molly listened at another door, and when looking inside she was greeted with a burst of daylight through a dusty window. She entered the room but found it empty. "Must be a spare room Malaban had nothing to put in," she thought. Though the room was barren and cold, the daylight cheered her. Molly deemed it safe to take a quick look outside. She pushed the hinged window open to let the cool winter air sweep in.

How it refreshed her! The castle air felt stale and damp, and Molly welcomed the sharp breeze that rushed over the plains and found its way to her. She inhaled deeply and leaned her chin on her arms and gazed out at the wintry landscape. Far away was a vast expanse of the dying brown plains, sprinkled with white patches of glistening snow. The icy waters of the moat lapped against the rocky shore below. She fondly recalled the winters back home, and thought there probably wasn't enough snow here to build a proper snowman.

When Molly glanced to her left, she saw a stone tower built in one corner of the castle, spiraling up into the crisp blue sky. Attached to a wooden pole on the roof of the tower was a huge black flag outlined with a blood red border. The flag of Malaban flapped noisily in the breeze. Molly noticed a tiny window near the top, and for an instant thought she caught a glimpse of a thin face peering out. Molly rubbed her eyes and looked again, but the face had vanished. She felt a little tired and thought her mind was playing tricks. Molly continued to watch the rolling plains and nearly drifted off to sleep till a sharp gust of wind pinched her face and brought her back to reality. "The rescue!" Molly closed the window at once and hurried out of the room, saddened to leave these untroubled moments behind.

"There you are," King Rupert said as Molly raced down the corridor to catch up with him. "I thought I was going to have to search for you too."

"Sorry. I was sort of daydreaming in one of the rooms. I looked outside. It's early morning right now."

"Then I'm doubly surprised that no one is up and about in the castle." King Rupert pondered the situation, then simply scratched his silver head of hair and sighed. "I do wish I knew what was going on. I hate being kept in the dark." He motioned to Molly. "Well, let's move on. Ulric is way ahead of us."

They had walked only a few yards when Ulric ran charging towards them. "Our luck has changed! I hear guards around the corner."

"We must flee to our hiding spot!" the king said.

"There's no time. We'll hide in this next room. Follow me!"

Ulric swung open a door and the trio rushed inside, and not a moment too soon. Seconds after Ulric closed the door, two trolls emerged from around the corner while on their patrol of the castle. Molly could hear their deep voices as they walked past the door. In time their conversation faded into the distance.

"That was close," the king said. "Fortunately those trolls didn't come in here." The king looked around. "Wherever *here* is."

The room they had hidden in was quite dark. A small torch fastened to the wall gave off very little light. The flame seemed ready to expire. After their eyes adjusted to the gloom, Ulric realized they were not in a room after all, but inside a cramped stairwell. A stone staircase spiraled above and below them. They stood on a small flat landing.

"I guess our luck is still with us," Ulric said. "I believe it is safe to continue." He placed his hand on the doorknob, ready to turn it, when he quickly stepped back into the shadows. "Wait! I hear voices again. They're coming back!"

King Rupert shook with fear. "They know we're here. It's all over. We're doomed, I tell you! We're doomed!"

"Quiet!" Ulric said. He then placed his ear to the door and wrinkled his brow in confusion. "I still hear voices." He looked up. "But they're not outside."

Ulric, Molly and King Rupert stood absolutely still and listened. Then very slowly, voices from below the staircase could be heard. They sounded harsh and disgruntled. "Troll voices," the king speculated. "Though one might be a goblin. It's hard to tell the difference sometimes."

"I hear them too," Molly said, nodding so that her ponytails danced on her shoulders. "I wonder what they're doing way down there."

"Let's leave at once," King Rupert said to Ulric.

But Ulric simply raised his hand for silence and continued to listen. The voices originated far below the castle, but were magnified as they drifted up the stone staircase, making the people sound closer than they actually were. Molly and the king watched with apprehension until Ulric looked up and smiled. "Luck is with us in abundance! I think we have found what we're after. From what I can make out of the conversation, those two individuals down there sound like prison guards."

"Meaning that the prison cells are right below us!" Molly concluded.

Any thought of turning back vanished immediately from King Rupert's mind. "Victory at last! Let's storm the prison and rescue Rosalind at once. I'll take on any troll or goblin without a second thought!"

Ulric tried to calm his king. "But we *must* take a second thought if we're to be successful. We can't rush our mission. One mistake and we're finished."

"You're right, of course," King Rupert said. "I'm getting way ahead of myself. I must take hold of my senses." He took a deep breath and exhaled.

"Feeling better?" Molly asked.

"A little. Now tell us what to do, Ulric."

Ulric gathered them around and whispered out his plan. "We will sneak downstairs and listen more carefully to determine just where we stand. Princess Rosalind may not be down there." The king frowned at the remark. "But if she is, I think we can overtake two guards, that is, if there are *only* two guards."

Ulric led the way, cautiously spiraling down the cold stone steps. The darkness increased at first since there were no torches along the way. As they neared the bottom, however, the light grew brighter. Before he knew it, Ulric stood on the last step looking straight ahead into the guardroom.

Luckily no guards were sitting at the small table in the corner. A mound of firewood was piled high next to it. A couple of empty mugs and bread crumbs were left on the table. The rest of the room was bare and lifeless.

Directly across the room from Ulric were two open doorways. One was wide and arched at the top, and Ulric could plainly see that it led to a gloomy corridor lined with a series of wooden doors with barred windows on each. Those were the prison cells. The other opening next to the archway was narrow and rectangular. Yellow light poured out from within it. This turned out to be the entrance to a small kitchen, the very place where the two voices originated. Ulric pointed in that direction and Molly and King Rupert understood. The trio continued to listen to the voices, now louder and clearer, yet hideous and frightful.

"Out of ale!" one shouted, definitely a troll's voice. "How can we be out of ale?"

"You just guzzled down the last of it!" the other snapped. He was certainly a goblin.

"Whoever stocks this pantry does a lousy job and should be thrown in the moat!" the troll complained. "Here we're stuck keeping guard and don't get enough food for a proper meal."

"Ever since Malaban disappeared, the *men* get all the privileges," the goblin snarled. "We get nothing!"

"Quit your yapping!" the troll said. "At least you have a storeroom to go to. I'm stuck up in that freezing cold tower keeping guard over my prisoner, without a slice of stale bread or a hunk of rabbit meat to keep me company. I have to climb all the way down here to find a bite to keep from starving!"

"I got a right to complain too! How would you like being stuck down in this hot awful cellar with nobody to talk to for hours?" the goblin asked. "All the company I get is your ugly face."

"Watch your mouth before I rip it off!"

"Can't you take a little ribbing? You trolls are so soft sometimes." The troll growled back at his fellow guard. "Oh, bury it!" the goblin continued. "Who knows, maybe us goblins and trolls won't make out so bad at the meeting. We deserve better treatment. Maybe Belthasar might finally realize that."

"I'll say we do!" the troll bellowed, slamming a fist against a cupboard door. "If we don't grab a good deal, then I'm running off the first chance I get. I'll live in the mountains again. At least there I'm my own boss."

"If an officer catches you away from your post, you'll be thrown into a cell yourself," the goblin said. "I'll end up guarding you!" he squealed with delight.

"Shut your ugly mouth!" the troll warned. "I'll get back to my post in plenty of time before anyone notices. Besides, that girl isn't going anyplace. The tower's locked up good and secure. I figure there's no harm in me taking a break. No one will find out."

The goblin grunted. "Suppose not. But at least you *have* a prisoner to guard. All my cells are empty. We haven't plundered a kingdom in an entire week! I'm bored sitting down here, waiting for them upstairs to march some genuine prisoners into my cells."

"There you go complaining again," the troll muttered. "Just give me that loaf of bread there. I'll wash it down with water. Humph! No ale. No warm guardroom. I *never* get a break!"

Ulric signaled to the king and Molly to retreat back up a few steps so they could talk. "Our friends in the pantry revealed some interesting pieces of information."

"The troll said he's guarding a girl in the tower. He had to be referring to Rosalind," King Rupert said, ready to run all the way up the stairs to the tower.

Ulric calmed the king. "First things first. We have to obtain the keys to unlock the tower prison. The troll guard surely has it with him."

That seemed quite a tall order, and King Rupert was afraid to ask what else had to be done. "And then?"

"Then we must make sure the troll and goblin are kept out of our way," Ulric said. "I don't know how long it will take to break into the tower. We can't have the troll returning before we are finished."

"How are we supposed to get the keys *and* get rid of the guards?" Molly inquired. "I don't see how the three of us can do all that."

Ulric didn't either at first, but slowly a plan took shape in his mind. He looked at Molly. "I think I know how we can accomplish it. And *you're* going to be the key to the entire plan."

"Me!" Molly truly wanted to help rescue Princess Rosalind, but to face a troll and a goblin in the process was something she never anticipated. "What can an eight-year-old girl do against those two monsters?"

Ulric hastily explained his idea, and though Molly still hadn't conquered her fear completely, her role in the operation wasn't as horrible as she first imagined. The three descended again, but Ulric and King Rupert remained hidden in the shadows of the last few steps. Molly ran across the guardroom and through the arched doorway leading to the row of prison cells. Then after waiting a moment to gather her courage, Molly started to whistle.

The notes were soft at first, then gradually grew louder and louder. Unfortunately not loud enough to attract the attention of the still bickering troll and goblin. Molly's fear soon turned into annoyance, so she stomped her foot and yelled out to the guards. "Hey, you two lunks in the kitchen! Get out here! I don't want to hang out in this revolting place forever!"

The troll's ears perked up. He shot out of the pantry and looked around, fearing that an officer may have discovered him away from his post in the tower. "Who said that?"

"Down here," Molly directed him. The troll glanced through the archway into the shadowy corridor with his beady red eyes. "That's better. Some guard you are, letting an itsy bitsy girl like me walk right past you!"

The troll scowled with embarrassment at first, then burst out laughing. The goblin in the pantry shouted out. "What's so funny?"

"We have an intruder," the troll replied, keeping a watchful eye on Molly.

"I'll get my club!"

"Don't bother," the troll said, still laughing till his sides ached. "Come out here and see what I found."

The goblin slipped out of the pantry and glanced through the archway, puzzled when seeing a little girl in his prison. His large eyes bulged out even more. "Who in blazes is she? And how'd she get in here?"

"Wouldn't you like to know," Molly taunted. "I ought to report you two for doing such a lousy job. You're all eating and arguing, and very little guarding. You couldn't guard your own shadows if you had to!"

The troll boiled at the remark and clenched his fists. "Is that so, little one? Well I'll show you who's guard and who's prisoner!" He exposed his sharp teeth then motioned to the goblin for assistance. "Let's grab her and lock her up!"

The two hulking figures slowly walked down the corridor towards Molly. Ulric now saw his chance to act, so he and King Rupert dashed across the floor and into the pantry. They quickly searched the small room and found what they needed—two weapons and a ring of keys. "One of these must go to the tower," Ulric said. "Quick! Take this sword." King Rupert grabbed the weapon. Ulric took the goblin's club standing in the corner. In the next instant they ran out of the room after the two guards, brandishing their weapons and hollering like wolves.

And not a moment too soon, for the troll and goblin were only a stone's throw away from Molly, ready to spring at her. "Try and get us instead!" Ulric shouted. "We're more your size than a little girl!"

The guards spun around and stared at the new intruders with mouths wide open and nostrils flaring. "They've got our weapons!" the goblin cried.

"And we'll use them if we must!" King Rupert said.

"You boys can't escape this way either," Molly added, grabbing a burning torch from the wall and waving it in front of the guards. "Give up, losers!"

The troll and goblin quickly realized they had been outwitted. Instantly their fierceness of a moment ago crumbled into cowardly obedience. Ulric hurriedly opened one of the prison cells and pushed the guards inside, then slammed the door shut and locked it.

"That should hold them for a while," Ulric said, leading the way back out of the corridor to the spiral staircase. "You were very brave, Molly. I wish some of my own troops possessed your courage and spirit."

Molly managed a suitable reply, not having the heart to tell Ulric that she had been scared right down to her socks. But that was behind her. Now a more important task confronted them as they hurried up the stairs two at a time. Molly, Ulric and King Rupert were swiftly closing in on finding Princess Rosalind.

CHAPTER TEN

A Rescue Gone Sour

"Won't these stairs ever come to an end?" Molly whispered miserably under her breath. Her heart beat wildly and her feet ached. King Rupert puffed and wheezed his way up to the tower with each clumsy footstep. Ulric held up best of all, though even he was visibly tired at times.

"If the trolls don't get us, exhaustion will!" the king said. "I'm too old for such athletics. A rest would do nicely right about now."

"No time," Ulric insisted. "We're so close to rescuing Princess Rosalind. Our small aches and pains can't compare to what she's been through."

King Rupert hadn't considered the situation in those terms and doubled his effort. "You're right, Ulric. I won't let a little pain keep me back. It will take a horde of trolls to stop me. Onward!"

King Rupert picked up his pace, climbing with renewed vigor and determination. But even that sudden burst of energy didn't last long, and he began to lag behind again. If they didn't reach the tower soon, he knew he wouldn't be able to go much farther. Then as all hope was nearly drained from his heart, Ulric spoke.

"The last step!"

King Rupert looked up as Ulric raced to the landing at the top. Molly and the king followed close behind, and soon the trio sat and rested on level ground. A door stood at the end of the narrow landing, but it would have to wait a moment for their tired limbs to recover.

Molly finally broke the silence. "I fear we may be followed. Shouldn't we go now? I'm feeling better."

"If anyone wants to follow us up those stairs, let them!" King Rupert said. "By the time they reach the top, they'll be too exhausted to raise a hand against us."

"Molly's right," Ulric said. "We've rested long enough." He stood and slowly opened the door. A gust of icy wind burst inside, refreshing him instantly. "We're at the top of the castle. A guard tower is directly in front. Princess Rosalind must be in there."

The king jumped to his feet when hearing the news. "Then what are we waiting for? Move on! Move on!"

The three walked through the door into the open air of morning. They stood on a narrow walkway with a stone railing jutting up on either side. To their right, stretching endlessly south, were the harsh plains they had traveled over. Molly could see the nearby woods where they had hidden before dawn. Below to the left was a huge courtyard with a large stone platform in the center and several concentric rings of benches around it.

"We must hurry," Ulric said as he led them along the walk to the guard tower in the corner of the castle. The whipping winds nearly threw them off balance. The black and red flag on top of the tower snapped in the biting breeze. Molly realized that the tower looked just like the one she had seen from the window downstairs. She wondered if she *had* seen a face peering out of it after all.

Ulric opened a door at the base of the tower and they entered, finding relief from the biting cold. Inside was damp and gloomy. A table and chair were squeezed into one corner of the room. "This is where that troll must have kept guard," King Rupert said. "But where's Rosalind?"

"Probably up above," Ulric said, pointing. "There's another staircase."

"How many stairs *are* there in this infernal place!" the king wailed.

"It's not steep like the other one," Molly said. "This tower isn't very high."

Ulric sprang up the staircase and Molly and King Rupert followed. Molly hadn't counted forty steps when Ulric spotted another door at the top.

"Please let this be the last door," the king said, reaching for the handle. He tried to open it. "Locked! We shall never get in!"

"Don't worry," Molly reminded the king. "Ulric has the keys, remember?"

Ulric produced the ring of keys he had swiped from the pantry, then began trying them one by one. The brass, silver and copper keys jingled with each attempt. "That troll has more keys than there are rooms in the castle."

"Oh, just hurry!" King Rupert pleaded. "My heart can't take much more strain."

"Another moment! Give me one more moment and I'll—ah ha!" Ulric shouted. He fitted a brass key into the lock and turned it. A sharp click sounded. The door unlocked.

King Rupert pushed the door open. It creaked painfully on its hinges, revealing a dim and musty room. A single window let in a stream of morning light. A small table below it contained an unlit candle and a basin of icy water. In the far corner of the room was an old battered bed. On it lay a pale thin figure, apparently lifeless amid the dreary surroundings.

The king walked cautiously into the room with Molly close by him. Ulric stepped inside, keeping watch at the door. King Rupert seemed afraid to approach the person on the bed, expecting the worse. Molly inched closer to the figure and saw a young lady with flowing blond hair and a beautiful face, though worn by fear and worry. Molly glanced at King Rupert, sensing his uneasiness.

"Is that your daughter?" she asked.

The king nodded, then walked up to Rosalind, certain he had arrived too late. He examined her face and closed eyes and nearly cried. Then he saw it. She was breathing! His heart leapt and he knelt at her side. "Rosalind," he said softly. "Wake up, Rosalind. Your father's here."

Slowly the young lady began to stir. Her eyes opened and she looked around in utter confusion, then in overwhelming joy. "Father? Is it really you?" Rosalind sat up and touched King Rupert's face till she knew he wasn't part of a lovely dream that would fade away. "It *is* you, father!" she cried, embracing him with all her might.

Quickly the color returned to her face, and Princess Rosalind looked as alive as a spring morning. Though still a bit shaken at the sight of her rescuers, she quickly told her father all that had happened since the attack on his castle so many days ago. Rosalind was glad to see Ulric standing by the door, but was at a loss for words when her eyes met with Molly's.

"I'm forgetting my manners," the king said with embarrassment. "You two do not know each other. Rosalind, this is Molly Jordan, a member of your rescue party. It's a long story which will have to wait for a better time."

"Pleased to meet you, Princess Rosalind," Molly said politely. "I'm so glad you're all right."

"Thank you, Molly," the princess replied. "And thank you for helping with my rescue. I never knew a girl so young who would risk her life in a place like this. I shall be happy to leave it."

Ulric stepped forward. "Then let us leave at once. I can imagine what an ordeal you've been through, Princess Rosalind, but we should go immediately while our way is still clear. I'm sorry I can't allow you time to rest."

"Do not apologize, Ulric. The sight of the three of you has renewed my strength." Princess Rosalind smiled for the first time in many days. "I am ready to depart at once. Not another minute in these awful surroundings!"

King Rupert was thrilled to see a fighting spirit in his daughter. He helped her to stand, and in a few moments the four scrambled down the stairs to the guard quarters below, then walked out the door and into the bright morning light. The cold air woke Princess Rosalind as she hurried along the stone walkway above the castle. The wind tossed her hair like waves of gold.

"It's wonderful to be outside again where there's life and light. I had nearly given up hope."

"Well we didn't," Molly assured the princess. "Especially your father. He wasn't about to give up no matter how difficult things were!"

King Rupert smiled at Molly for her kind words. The worry and despair of the last few days washed out of him instantly. He felt as if he had the spirit and strength to fly right off the castle wall into the wintry blue sky.

Finally they reached the door entering into the main section of the castle. "Not those horrid stairs again!" the king grumbled.

"They'll be much easier going down," Ulric assured him. "Just don't rush too fast. Trip once and you might end up spiraling to the bottom. And taking us with you!"

Everyone descended swiftly but cautiously in single file. They reached the landing on the main floor of the castle in less than half the time it took going up. They now stood at the spot where they had first heard the voices of the troll and goblin guards from the prisons below.

"I hope our two friends are still secure in the cells," the king said. "We'd be in an awful mess if they ever escaped."

"We've been safe up to this point. Let me listen into the corridor to see if all is clear inside the castle," Ulric said. He placed his ear to the door.

"Anything?" Molly asked.

"Dead quiet," he said. "That worries me."

"Do we stay or go?" the king asked impatiently. "If you don't hear anything, I say that's good. Let's go!"

"Very well." Ulric opened the door to find the castle corridor deserted.

"Free at last!" the king cheered. "This way, all of you. I'll lead you back to our hiding place by the moat."

King Rupert led the others, certain their way would be unhindered. Ulric, Molly and Princess Rosalind swiftly followed. Soon the king approached a corner and prepared to turn it without so much as a cautious look beforehand. Ulric tried to stop him, but it was too late. King Rupert bounded around the corner. His face quickly contorted into expressions of horror as he found himself and his followers barreling towards an angry mob of troll and goblin soldiers.

"Retreat!" Ulric shouted.

The four of them had just enough time to stop before crashing into the soldiers. But before they could turn around to run the opposite way, another group of soldiers rushed at them from behind. Each troll and goblin squad closed in on the unarmed intruders like spiders stalking flies caught in a web. King Rupert felt the life drain back out of him. He had led his people head first into a trap, and there was no escape.

The troll whom they had imprisoned below stepped forward, his leathery flesh looking sinister in the flickering torchlight. "So you thought you outsmarted us," he sneered, keeping an eye on King Rupert all the while. "Well nobody breaks into our castle without paying the consequences!" The other guards hooted and cheered.

"I say we throw them in the moat!" the goblin guard said. "No one locks me in my own prison and gets away with it." He walked up to Ulric. "You forgot to take *these*," he snickered, dangling a ring of keys in front of his face. "I keep a spare set hidden under my vest. Your rescue plan never had a chance!"

Jeers and shouts again erupted, and it took some time before the troll could settle the troops. "Quiet! Quiet! I've already decided what to do with our prisoners. I'll show them who is really in control around here. Bind their hands!"

Swiftly, four soldiers rushed forward, one to each prisoner, and tied their hands behind their backs. Molly kicked one of the trolls in the shin, but only hurt her toes in the process. The troll didn't feel a thing through its thick hide.

"You won't get away with this injustice!" King Rupert bellowed. "First you kidnap my daughter, and now me and my followers. No indeed, you will not get away with it!"

"But we already have!" the goblin howled. "In this castle, you live by our rules!"

"Enough merrymaking," the troll said. "There'll be plenty of time for that later on. First things first." He clapped his hands and a group of soldiers surrounded the prisoners. The others lined up behind them. The troll walked up front and signaled for all to follow him. "This way, little mice," he said to the prisoners. "Your sentences await."

"Where are you taking us?" Molly demanded. Fear and anger churned inside her, and she wanted to rush at one of the guards and knock him down. But Molly held back, not wanting any harm to befall her friends because of her own reckless actions.

"You'll know very soon," the troll replied, letting out a chilling laugh that made Molly quiver. "Oh yes, you will all know your miserable fate very soon!"

CHAPTER ELEVEN

A Recipe For Sleep

Molly hadn't the foggiest idea where they were being taken, but was certain it would probably be an unpleasant place. She was rushed along winding passageways with the others, for the troll in charge had commanded his soldiers to move as fast as possible. Molly's legs were tired and her wrists ached from the rope biting into her skin.

"How are you holding up, Molly?" Princess Rosalind whispered. "I'm sorry I landed you in all this trouble. Maybe it would have been better not to rescue me at all. At least the rest of you would be safe then."

"Don't say such things, Princess Rosalind. We'll find a way out. We've gone to too much trouble to rescue you to have everything end like this."

"Quit that whispering, you vermin!" one of the soldiers yelled. "Pay attention to where you're going. Don't make us gag you too."

Molly heeded the warning and remained silent. But her thoughts were still busy determining every possible way of breaking free.

At last they reached the end of their tiresome journey as the troll ordered his soldiers to stop. King Rupert and the others looked around, happy that they hadn't been taken to a dungeon as expected. Instead, the group stood outside of an enormous pair of

wooden doors on which were carved pictures of dragons and ser-
pents and vultures. The troll instructed two soldiers to open them.

"Now you will face your doom!" he said with glee.

The four prisoners were ushered into an enormous hall filled
with hundreds of men, trolls and goblins seated at large tables
spread throughout the room. Molly's hopes for escape were dashed
at once.

The troll ran up to a platform situated at one end of the chamber. Seated at a table on it were the castle's highest officers. "We
have a gift for you!" he shouted, motioning for his soldiers to escort the prisoners over. Molly, King Rupert, Princess Rosalind and
Ulric were brought right up to the platform and presented before
Belthasar.

"And who have we here?" Belthasar asked.

"Prisoners!" the troll replied. "Four intruders who were not
clever enough to escape under my watch."

In fact, these were the very four prisoners that Christopher
had seen from atop the balcony while spying with Artemas and
Mr. Smithers. They were watching now, shocked that their friends
had been captured, and at a loss as to how to rescue them from the
turmoil below.

"What do you wish to do with them?" the troll asked.

Belthasar thought for a moment, then walked to the edge of
the platform. "What a surprise this is! I believe we have the great
King Rupert of Endora before us, though at the moment he doesn't
appear so great." All the troops gathered in the chamber jeered
and hissed.

"You'll pay for this!" the king snapped. "Malaban may have
left you in charge, but I'll see you get what's coming to you, you
scoundrel!"

"My dear King," Belthasar said. "I am not the only one in
charge. I have just decided to let Arga and Crull assist me in running this castle." He pointed to the troll and goblin seated at the
table. "In fact, I was just about to announce my Great Plan. But I
think your presence sheds a new light on matters."

"What are you talking about?" King Rupert said. He had nearly reached his boiling point.

"All in good time," Belthasar replied. He then turned to address the crowd. "I have decided to postpone the announcement of my Great Plan." There were groans of disappointment. "However, I *will* announce it tonight in the castle courtyard. With the arrival of King Rupert and his companions, I must make a few changes in my plan before I make it known." This is what everyone wanted to hear. They applauded Belthasar by stomping their feet and pounding their fists on the tables.

"Shall I take them to the prisons?" the troll guard asked after the noise died down.

"In a moment. First I want to ask King Rupert a simple question. Where is our leader Malaban?"

The room was so silent that you could hear the snapping of the torch flames. King Rupert scowled at Belthasar. "I know nothing of Malaban's whereabouts. Your leader is of no concern to me."

Belthasar grew angry at the response, but let it stand. "Very well. If you claim to know nothing of Malaban's disappearance, I will believe you. For now. But enough of this!" He signaled to the troll. "Take these intruders to the prison! I'll deal with them later tonight in the courtyard." The troll ordered his guards around the prisoners and had them hastily escorted out of the chamber.

"We're in trouble now," Molly whispered to the king. "What do you think they'll do to us? And what's this *Great Plan* Belthasar spoke of? I don't like him. He looks like an ugly scarecrow."

"I don't like him either. And I wish I knew what he was up to, though I'm sure it's no good." King Rupert sighed in distress as they marched through a passageway. "I only hope Artemas, Christopher and Mr. Smithers are faring better than we are. They may be our last hope!"

High up on the balcony, Christopher shuddered at the spectacle just played out before him. "We have to go after them!" he frantically whispered to Artemas. "They have my sister!"

"I'm well aware of that. But let's go back inside the stairwell before we discuss things further. My bones are starting to ache lying cramped up here on the floor."

Quietly and carefully, the trio crawled back through the door and closed it. The noisy voices of the men, trolls and goblins below lessened as the gathering adjourned and they exited the meeting hall. Artemas then realized that the castle would be crawling with the enemy at any moment. He feared that their way back to the hiding place or to the prisons to make a rescue would be blocked.

"What should we do now?" Mr. Smithers asked. "Princess Rosalind was apparently rescued with no help from us. But now she has been captured again—along with her rescuers! If we're not careful, we'll be next."

"That would be disastrous," Artemas said.

Christopher agreed. "The last place I want to be is stuck in a prison cell, especially with no one left outside to save me." He looked over at the magician blanketed in the shadows. "Tell us what to do, Artemas."

"First we get back down to the main level of the castle. No use in waiting up here like frightened birds in a nest," he said. "Then we'll return to our hiding place by the moat if we can. Since the meeting has ended, we may have to wait there awhile till things settle down."

"That will give us a chance to plan a rescue," Christopher suggested. "I hope Molly and the others are treated kindly."

"I hope they don't accidentally tell the guards that there are three more of us running loose in the castle," Mr. Smithers said. "Bad enough we have to hide like church mice. We don't need a search party after us too."

RES

The journey down the spiral staircase proved much easier than the one going up. As Artemas approached the last two turns in the staircase, he thought he detected voices near the bottom. He halted, placing a finger to his lips. Christopher and Mr. Smithers understood and stopped, keeping absolutely still as Artemas silently walked down the few remaining steps. Waiting at the bottom of the stairs were two large and vicious-looking trolls armed with wooden clubs. They were the very same trolls who had searched Malaban's chamber earlier that morning. Artemas nearly ran into them as he rounded the last curve in the staircase.

"Ah ha!" one of the trolls cried when spotting Artemas. "Didn't I tell you I heard voices in Malaban's chamber, Bolo?"

"You were right, Nagg! Captain Urgot will reward us for capturing him!"

But Artemas didn't want to give them the chance. He was still a few feet from the trolls, so before they could spring at him, the magician leaped backwards up a few steps and waited.

"Seems I'm too quick for a couple of lazy trolls!" Artemas taunted.

"Call *us* lazy, will you!" Nagg seethed with anger. "Run all the way up those stairs if you want, old man, but we'll catch you. There's no way out from the top."

Artemas thought for a moment, keeping his eyes on the trolls, then nodded. "You're probably right," he said, loudly enough so Christopher and Mr. Smithers could hear him. They were still safely hidden in the shadows farther up the staircase. "I might as well give myself up instead of trying to escape by climbing all these stairs again. They're too tiring."

Mr. Smithers was startled that Artemas seemed willing to give up so easily. Christopher assured him that the magician probably had some plan of escape in mind and to play along.

"Now you're talking sense," Nagg said. "If you give up all nice and quiet, it'll be much easier on you."

"All right," Artemas said as the trolls approached the first step. "Just tell me where you'll take me."

Nagg and Bolo looked at each other and grinned. "To the dungeon, of course! What a dumb question," Bolo said. "Where'd you think we'd take you?"

The magician looked surprised. "Did you say—*take the vial of blue liquid out of the cloth sack?*" he said loudly.

The trolls paused and scratched their heads in confusion. They hadn't the slightest idea what Artemas meant. But Christopher did. He untied the sack of articles from his belt that Artemas had gathered in Malaban's chamber and quickly searched through it. He removed a small glass vial half filled with a dark blue liquid.

"What are you talking about?" Nagg complained.

"He's trying to confuse us!" Bolo said. "Let's grab him before he makes a run for it."

"Oh, I won't run off," Artemas said. "I gave you my word. I simply wanted to know where you'd be taking me."

"And I told you!" Bolo grumbled.

"Did you?" Artemas said. "I thought you said—*find the vial of red liquid and mix it with the blue!*"

The magician's trickery proved too much for the trolls. "Get down those stairs now!" Nagg shouted at the top of his lungs. "Or we'll go up there and drag you down by your collar! We're not going to listen to your nonsense!"

"All right! All right! I'll do as you ask." Slowly Artemas descended the last few steps, first one, then another, then a third, till he was nearly within the trolls' grasp. He lifted his foot as if ready to take one more step, then turned and bolted back up the spiral staircase, leaving Nagg and Bolo sputtering at his escape.

"After him!" Nagg cried.

Artemas had climbed twenty steps before the lumbering trolls had even begun to chase him. When he reached Christopher and Mr. Smithers farther up, he clapped his hands in joy, for Christopher had understood his deception with the trolls and had mixed the vials of blue and red liquid. He handed the mixture to Artemas.

"What will that do?" Christopher asked.

"Watch and see!" Artemas hurled the glass vial down the steps. A second or two lapsed before they heard the shattering of glass. "Quick! Back to the top of the stairs! We'll be safe if we're higher up."

The trio puffed and panted their way up the steps till Artemas deemed it was safe to stop. He paused to listen to the trolls below.

"I don't hear a thing," Mr. Smithers said. "Have they stopped chasing us?"

"If my plan was successful, they have. Follow me."

They climbed back down the stairs for a second time until their way was blocked by the two trolls. There they were, sprawled out upon the steps, fast asleep and snoring loud enough to wake the dead. The glass vial lay nearby in a dozen pieces.

"Did those colorful liquids do *that*?" Mr. Smithers asked in amazement.

Artemas chuckled. "I had to think quickly, and a sleeping potion was all that came to mind. The initial burst from the mixture has dissipated, so we're safe. But those two will be out for a few hours at least."

"Then let's get out of here," Christopher said. "I don't want to look at those trolls for another second."

Artemas agreed and was about to head for the door, when he looked at Mr. Smithers for a moment then studied the two trolls. "You're almost about the size of the smaller troll, Mr. Smithers."

"More or less. So?"

"I think I have a plan."

"What have *I* got to do with it?" he grumbled.

"No time for questions. Just help me get a uniform off this troll. I'll explain everything as we go along," Artemas said.

Mr. Smithers wanted an explanation then and there, but realized that each moment they remained, the worse their danger grew. So without another word, they quickly removed the troll's uniform then slipped back out into the castle corridors. They only had to dodge one guard on the way to their hiding spot. Unfortunately, after they were back inside safe and secure, the guard returned, passing by their doorway every several minutes while on his patrol.

"We may be stuck in here awhile." Artemas sighed. "Now that the castle is alive again, our chances of roaming about freely are diminished. I think we'll have to wait till nightfall to attempt a rescue. By then the guard might leave. Besides, we all need some sleep."

Christopher missed Molly and hoped that she wasn't frightened. "What do you think will happen tonight at that meeting Belthasar spoke of?"

"I wish I knew," Artemas said. "But you can bet it won't be anything good."

The answer brought little comfort to Christopher. He walked to the door overlooking the moat and peered out of the barred window. The mid morning skies shone clear and bright. He felt a slight breeze on his face. But inside it was damp, dark and miserable. Christopher slumped down on the floor and recalled the night he and Molly were sitting in the museum hallway. He wished they were back there now so he could take his sister home where she belonged. A part of him regretted walking through the timedoor without thinking about it first. If only he had the power to change things. Christopher looked around his cramped quarters and leaned his head wearily against the wall. He felt just as much a prisoner here as Molly certainly did somewhere far off in the castle.

CHAPTER TWELVE

The Great Plan

The minutes passed like hours as they rested. There was little to do except sit and think or look out of the door across the moat, all which grew quite tedious after the first hour. At one point Christopher listened by the door at the top of the stairs and heard the guard in the hallway talking to someone about the meeting later that night. One of the men referred to three other intruders running loose through the castle. Christopher realized that he, Artemas and Mr. Smithers were those very intruders.

"We've been discovered," he informed the others. "No doubt a search party is combing every inch of this castle for our whereabouts."

"Probably," Artemas said without much concern. He yawned and sat on the floor. "Our sleeping trolls must have awakened and reported us. But I think we're safe. With a guard patrolling right outside our door, who would even *think* to search in here?"

Christopher hoped the magician was right as he found another place to sit. He grew weary of the boredom that plagued them and felt as cooped up as a chicken in a pen. Christopher longed to run out of the castle and race across the plains with the wind at his back, but he knew that was not possible. Thinking about it only made him feel worse. So as the hours dragged by, and seeing there was no business to attend to yet, each one finally drifted off to sleep.

Christopher opened his eyes to total darkness. "What's going on?" he thought in a panic. His senses confused him, so he jumped up and looked out of the window in the door. The night sky was dotted with fiery white stars. The three of them had slept through the entire day!

Christopher tiptoed up the stairs and listened at the doorway. He heard nothing in the corridor—no talking and no steady footsteps of a patrolling guard. Christopher hoped the man had left his post. He held his breath and slowly opened the door a crack. To his relief, the passageway was empty. He ran to wake his friends.

"Artemas! Mr. Smithers! Get up. It's after dark and our guard is gone."

Artemas stirred and grumbled, his back sore from leaning against the stone wall. "What's all the commotion? What—what happened to the light?"

"It's night already. We slept through the day."

"Impossible!"

Mr. Smithers opened his eyes and stretched. "Well we certainly needed the rest. I don't suppose we have any food. I could stand a proper meal about now."

"There's no time for food," Christopher said, urging them to get up. "The guard left his post, so now's our chance to go and rescue the others!"

Artemas agreed. "I hope I remember where the prison cells are located. It's a good thing you found that map room, Christopher, otherwise we might be searching this place for hours."

Artemas and Christopher were ready to leave when Mr. Smithers paused at the bottom of the stairs. "Excuse me if this sounds like a dumb remark, Artemas, but you never told us *how* we're going to rescue the others. We can't walk in the prison and politely ask the guards to release our friends."

"On the contrary. We *will* walk right in. And you, Mr. Smithers, will lead us there."

"Me! Why me?"

"Because you will be wearing the guard uniform we took from that troll."

"I almost forgot about that." Mr. Smithers grabbed the uniform and tried it on. The pants and shirt were made of a dark coarse material which was very uncomfortable to wear. An animal skin vest topped it off. "So how do I look?"

"Very silly," Christopher laughed. "But I think you'll pass for a guard."

"So do I," Artemas said. "By now my plan is obvious. We'll walk to the prisons. If anyone stops us on the way, Mr. Smithers can say he captured us and is going to deliver us to the prison warden."

Mr. Smithers complimented the magician. "Very clever. Just one thing. What do we do once we get inside, assuming we ever get that far?"

Artemas shrugged his shoulders. "At this moment, Mr. Smithers, your guess is as good as mine." So with that bit of discouraging news, they departed.

To their relief, they found no difficulty reaching the door that led downstairs to the prison cells. All the passageways were again deserted just as at dawn. Artemas opened the door to reveal a dimly lit stairway, the very same one where Molly, King Rupert and Ulric had heard the voices of the troll and goblin guard. All was now silent. Artemas led the others down the spiral stairs and into the guard room. There they saw the archway leading to the cells and the second doorway going into the pantry. Everything was still eerily quiet.

"The place is deserted," Mr. Smithers whispered. "Let's have a look around."

Artemas poked his head through the pantry door. "Nobody's in here. Let's look inside all the cells."

One by one, Christopher, Mr. Smithers and the magician

looked inside each prison cell, only to find them cold and empty. Christopher even called out Molly's name, but there was no answer. At the far end of the corridor, Mr. Smithers found an iron door, but it was locked.

"I suppose we're too late," Mr. Smithers said as the trio walked back into the main guard room.

Artemas began to pace, fearing that all of his planning had been in vain. "If only we hadn't fallen asleep! We might have arrived here in time. Our friends have probably been taken to the meeting in the courtyard that Belthasar has planned."

Christopher's hope sank. "We'll never be able to rescue them from that location. Hundreds of soldiers will be gathered there like flies!"

"Looks like we're back where we started," Mr. Smithers sadly acknowledged. "It was a good try though."

"We can't give up yet!" Artemas said. "At least let's go to the courtyard to see what's happening. We may not be able to rescue them, but we can check if they're all right. We owe them that much at least."

"If you're not giving up," Christopher said, "then I certainly won't. Lead the way, Artemas!"

So the rescuers hurried back to the main floor of the castle. Between them, they were able to determine where the courtyard was located from what they could remember of the map. Soon they heard the steadily growing clamor of human, troll and goblin voices in the distance. After turning a corner in another passage, they saw ahead of them a wide brick hallway stretching on for about twenty yards. At the far end stood two mammoth doors, both wide open, revealing the outdoor courtyard of the castle which was filled with soldiers. The chilly night air swept inside and made Christopher shiver.

"Here we are," Mr. Smithers said anxiously. "Now what? We can't just walk down there and go outside."

"Not unless you want to be taken prisoner," Artemas said. He glanced down to the other end of the passage. "I think I see a guard standing outside by each door. Luckily they're paying attention to the meeting and not facing our direction."

"Do you think Belthasar announced his Great Plan yet?" Christopher asked. "I expect what's *great* for him would be *disastrous* for us."

"I'm inclined to agree with you." Artemas considered their options. "We have two choices. We can run back to our hiding place and hope that King Rupert and the others are taken to the prisons. Maybe we can attempt another rescue later."

"What's our second choice?" Mr. Smithers asked, though a part of him didn't want to find out.

"Our second alternative is to approach the main doors by the courtyard and try to listen in on the meeting."

"That's ridiculous!" Mr. Smithers said. "We're surely to be spotted if either of those guards turn around."

"That's a chance we have to take," Artemas said. "But notice the two doors down there. They open into the castle towards us. If we stay with our backs to the wall, we'll be concealed in the shadows just enough to sneak down there, hide behind the open doors and listen in. We've got to hear what they're going to do to our friends. We'll leave before the meeting is over."

Mr. Smithers shook his head. "I say it's risky."

"What other choice is there?" Christopher said. "We can't keep waiting for second chances. We may never get another. I say we try it."

After some quiet debating, Mr. Smithers finally gave in and agreed to the magician's plan. Artemas led the way down the passage, staying as close to the brick wall as possible. They quickly neared the doors—another ten yards and they would be safe. Then their hopes were dashed. As the voices outside in the courtyard grew in volume, another set of voices inside the castle seemed to be getting closer. A band of soldiers was swiftly approaching.

"We're trapped!" Mr. Smithers said frantically. "I knew we should have gone back. Now what?"

"I thought everyone was already at the meeting!" Artemas said. "We haven't much time. Mr. Smithers, I hope you can act."

"Act? Me! What do I have to do?"

"You're dressed like a castle guard, remember? Now lead Christopher and me back up this corridor as if we're your prisoners. And try to look angry."

Artemas and Christopher walked back in the direction they had come from, with Mr. Smithers behind them, acting the part of their guard. Soon a group of soldiers turned the corner, led by a particularly large and gruesome troll.

"Move on!" Mr. Smithers shouted at the first sight of the patrol. "We haven't all day, you know!"

When the troll saw the trio approach, he ordered his troops to halt. "Just what have we here?" he asked as Artemas and Christopher neared.

"These are two of the other intruders that were reported," Mr. Smithers said as convincingly as he could. He hoped he appeared grim and unfeeling, but inside he was as scared as a mouse. "I just caught the sneaks trying to spy on Belthasar's meeting. What shall I do with them?"

The troll smiled wickedly, his pointed yellow teeth glaring in the dim light. "Excellent work, soldier! And you've captured these hideous spies single-handedly. Belthasar will hear of your accomplishment." He looked sharply at Christopher and Artemas. "What do you two have to say for yourselves? Speak up!"

"We were trying to help our friends!" Christopher said angrily. "Who do you think you are anyway?"

"I'm the one in charge, little worm!" the troll scoffed. "And you're my prisoner." He laughed and signaled for Mr. Smithers to join his group. "We're going to the meeting and will escort your prisoners there. They will join their friends in the festivities!" he howled, prompting the other soldiers to jeer at the captives.

Not knowing what else to do, Mr. Smithers fell in line with the other soldiers and was soon marching towards the courtyard. Artemas and Christopher were kept up front with their hands tied behind them. The troll in charge even confiscated the small sack of potions that Artemas had given to Christopher for safekeeping. No magic would save them this time. Though Christopher couldn't imagine what would happen to him now, he was grateful that he would soon see Molly. If anything, they would be able to talk to each other before their doom was pronounced.

Belthasar howled in delight at the sight of the two prisoners entering the courtyard. Christopher and Artemas were taken onto a platform in the center. The night air was cold and blustery. There to greet them, downtrodden and grim, were Molly, King Rupert, Princess Rosalind and Ulric.

"I see you've decided to join our little party," the king whispered to Artemas.

"We didn't have a choice. But at least Mr. Smithers is still free. He may be able to help us yet."

"Good thing he tagged along on our journey." But the king said no more for Belthasar was about to speak.

Belthasar stood at the edge of the platform as the swarm of soldiers circled about. The stars above dropped their icy light. "First we had four prisoners, and now six!" he shouted to a chorus of rousing cheers. "But I'll deal with them in a moment. First to the business at hand—the announcement of my Great Plan!"

Thunderous applause flooded the courtyard. Christopher hardly paid attention as he edged his way over to Molly. "Are you all right?" he asked. "I'm sorry our rescue didn't work out."

"That's okay, Chris. At least you're here. That makes me feel much better." Molly sighed and tried to hold back some tears. "I wonder what Mom and Dad are doing now. And little Vergil. How I miss them!"

"So do I."

"What if we never see them again?"

Christopher tried to comfort his little sister. "Don't give up hope, Molly, no matter how awful things appear. We're not beaten yet."

"Stop talking!" one of the soldiers shouted. "Listen to what Belthasar has to say."

Christopher wanted to lash out at the soldier, but thought it best not to provoke him. He listened as the Great Plan was announced.

Belthasar strutted back and forth along the platform with his hands clasped together. "My Great Plan is this! In three days, every soldier in this castle will assemble on the plains at the front gate. Then at my command, we will ride together till we reach King Rupert's castle in Endora. We will overtake his entire kingdom, and this time we will not fail! We will defeat our enemy once and for all!"

If a thunder and lightning storm had erupted above the castle at that instant, nobody would have noticed because of all the noise the soldiers were making. They stomped and shouted with furious excitement, and voiced their eagerness for the battle to be waged.

"You will never defeat my people!" King Rupert shouted after the noise had settled. "Though I may be your prisoner, my troops in Endora will not fall!"

Belthasar laughed. "My men outnumber yours by the hundreds. The only reason Malaban didn't defeat you the last time is because he wasn't smart enough to fight with all of his soldiers. I will come prepared for battle. Your reign over Endora will soon end!"

"And what do you intend to do with us?" Princess Rosalind demanded to know. "You kidnapped me once and I escaped. Don't think you can keep me locked up for a second time!"

Belthasar smirked. "I can be a generous man. So I will let *you* decide your own fate." King Rupert and the others were stunned. "I will give you two choices. One—you can remain imprisoned here in my dungeon forever!"

"That's not much of a choice," King Rupert said. "What's your alternative? Though I'm sure it will be as laughable as the first."

"Your second choice is this. I will set you free," he said, pausing to see the wide-eyed amazement on their faces. "I will set you all free—*if* you assist me in defeating Endora!"

King Rupert's jaw dropped. "That is an outrageous sugges-tion, Belthasar! I will never attack my own kingdom."

"Certainly not!" Artemas said. "We will remain loyal to our king to the end."

"You bet we will!" Christopher added, accompanied by a nod of support from Molly.

Belthasar pondered their answer for a moment, then shook his head. "You have made a terrible mistake. I offer you freedom, but you choose imprisonment for the rest of your lives. Is that your final decision?"

"Only a dishonorable soul like you would expect any other," King Rupert said.

"So be it!" Belthasar stepped off the platform and signaled to the soldiers who had brought the new prisoners in. "Take these six intruders to the vault below the castle and lock them inside. Let them *never* see the light of day again!" The soldiers quickly sur-rounded King Rupert and the others and ushered them out of the courtyard. Mr. Smithers went with them, pretending to jeer at the prisoners as the other soldiers were doing. "Enjoy your stay," Belthasar called out to King Rupert as he left, "because you're going to be stuck here for a very, *very* long time!"

CHAPTER THIRTEEN

Another Rescue

The six captives were rushed through the castle corridors, then down to the prisons in the lower level. After reaching the guard-room, they passed underneath the archway leading to the row of prison cells. "I don't suppose we'll get a cell with a sunset view," King Rupert joked, trying to raise the spirits of his companions.

The troll in charge heard his comment and roared with laughter. "You'll never *see* another sunset where you're going!"

The soldiers marched them past each prison cell to the back of the corridor. There they halted in front of the iron door that Mr. Smithers had noticed on his first visit. The troll guard grabbed a torch from the wall then unlocked the door with a large key. He ordered another troll to open it. The darkness inside was suffocating. The prisoners were herded down a winding narrow staircase.

Down, down it twisted, going so far below the castle that the air grew cold and stale. There wasn't a single window anywhere. The only light came from the troll's wildly flickering torch. At last they reached the bottom. King Rupert and Artemas puffed and panted at the end of their tiring descent. Ulric and Princess Rosalind were also tired but said nothing. Christopher and Molly simply felt alone and unwanted.

The bottom of the steps opened into a small room which was as black as the night sky. A few soldiers grabbed some torches on the wall and lit them with the one the troll held. Soon the room was ablaze in an eerie red and yellow glow, revealing an empty stone room with an iron door built into one of the walls. A round metal wheel protruded from the center of the door which controlled the locking mechanism. At the chief guard's signal, a short, bulky goblin walked to the door and began to turn the wheel. A sliding bolt grumbled inside the door. Finally the wheel produced a dull clanking sound and stopped turning. The goblin pulled at the wheel with all his strength till the heavy door slowly opened. The air seemed even darker inside if that was possible.

"Here is where you'll spend the rest of your lives!" the troll guard said. "I hope you find your quarters enjoyable."

"More enjoyable than your presence!" King Rupert snapped back. "But don't think that you have heard the last of me!"

"Oh, I think I have." He motioned to his troops. "Untie them. Those ropes won't be necessary now. There is no escape from the vault."

When Princess Rosalind's hands were untied, she ran up to the chief guard. "At least let the children go!" she pleaded. "They are so young. They don't deserve this cruel fate."

"Stand back!" he warned. "The children will receive the same punishment as everyone else. No exceptions!"

"Don't be afraid for us, Princess Rosalind," Christopher said. "Molly and I won't abandon any of you."

"We're here till the very end," Molly added.

Princess Rosalind gazed at the children with both pride and sadness. "How brave such young people can be in the face of evil. It is an honor to know you both." She gently kissed Molly and Christopher on the forehead. "There is more courage within the two of you than in all the soldiers and generals in this miserable place."

"Enough!" the troll shouted. "You've had your say. Now get into the vault! All of you!"

The soldiers shoved the six prisoners inside the chilling blackness of the vault. They watched helplessly as the goblin who had opened the door, slowly closed it with a sinister laugh. The light from the torches outside the door grew dimmer and dimmer till they were entombed in darkness. They heard the wheel being turned. The bolt inside creaked and rumbled till the door was securely locked. All was now deathly quiet. They were trapped. Trapped forever beneath the castle in utter darkness and despair, without the slightest hope of escape.

No one spoke for what seemed the longest time. The dreadful finality of the situation had numbed their senses. Molly finally managed a few words.

"Is everyone here? I can't see a thing."

"We're here," King Rupert assured her. "That's all we seem capable of doing—just being here. Without any light, our plight is hopeless. And who knows how long the air inside will last."

"I might be able to help," Artemas spoke up. "If I had some wood, I may be able to start a fire."

"It'll take a bit of doing, but if we all feel around we might turn up something," Ulric said. "Just be careful so you don't run into each other."

Everyone searched about, though at first it seemed like a madhouse. People stumbled and bumped against one another, and there were a few stubbed toes as well. King Rupert finally directed each person to a separate area of the chamber to search it.

"The floor and walls are stone," Christopher said. "So I guess we can't dig our way out."

Suddenly Princess Rosalind shouted. "I found a piece of wood on the wall! It feels charred at the top. Probably an old torch."

"Bring it to me. I'm over here," Artemas said.

Rosalind found the magician and handed him the torch. "I hope you can start a fire, Artemas."

"I hope my magic works this far under the ground."

Everyone held their breath in anticipation of some light to brighten the dismal surroundings. Artemas didn't disappoint them. In an instant, a blue and yellow flash shot up to the ceiling like lightning. Artemas now stood there holding a flaming torch. The darkness dispersed and King Rupert began to inspect their prison.

The vault was low and circular, about thirty feet in diameter. It had been dug out of the rock, and loose stones were still scattered about. At a few points along the ground lay the remains of three or four skeletons, their bones slowly decaying to dust. Molly nearly screamed when she spotted them.

"Seems we aren't the first prisoners to be locked away here," Ulric grimly commented. "Those poor fellows have probably been trapped inside here for years."

"I hope we don't end up like that," Molly said. "There must be a way out!"

King Rupert tapped on the vault door and sighed. "I'm afraid not, Molly. We're trapped."

Christopher ran over to Artemas. "Why can't you open the door with magic? You unlocked the door by the moat to get us inside the castle."

Artemas examined the door and frowned. "This door is too large, too heavy and securely locked. Why, it would take all of my strength just to move the bolt inside a mere fraction of an inch. The door I opened to get inside the castle had only a tiny lock. And even *that* taxed my powers at the time." Artemas sat on the ground. "There's another reason why I can't open the door," he added.

"What is it?" Molly inquired.

"I sense that a magic spell has been cast upon the door. No doubt Malaban placed the spell on it himself when he had this vault constructed. Probably as a precaution to keep people like me from escaping."

"Just our luck!" Christopher muttered.

"So even if I had the strength to open it with magic, I wouldn't be able to override a sorcerer's spell." Artemas shook his head in defeat. "King Rupert is right. We're trapped!"

In the meantime, the troop of soldiers outside the vault retreated up the stairs, celebrating their victory over King Rupert and his friends. Mr. Smithers stayed in back of the group, hoping to run away as soon as he had the chance. After marching out through the guardroom and back up to the main level of the castle, the troll in charge dismissed the soldiers. They quickly scattered in all directions. Now it was late into the night and most of them would be retiring after a busy day.

Mr. Smithers followed two goblin soldiers from a safe distance, not knowing where else to go. He still wasn't familiar with this section of the castle. After passing through several corridors, his eyes lit up when finally spotting a place he knew well—his kitchen. As soon as the two soldiers were a good way ahead of him, Mr. Smithers slipped inside the empty room and closed the door. He was safe at last.

"My kitchen!" he whispered to himself. "Now I know which part of the castle I'm in. What luck! I haven't eaten since this morning."

Mr. Smithers gobbled up a few crusts of bread lying on one of the counters and drank some water from the barrel in the corner. For dessert he helped himself to the apples in the sacks along the wall. After having his fill, he knew the others would be hungry when he rescued them. "*If* I rescue them," he wondered. "How will I ever get back to that vault?"

The answer to that question had to wait. For now he emptied one of the apple sacks about halfway so it was light enough to carry. Mr. Smithers also gathered every last scrap of bread he could find and placed them in the sack with the apples. "Not the fanciest meal," he thought, "but it's better than starving."

Slinging the apple sack over his shoulder, Mr. Smithers left the kitchen and found his way back to the hideout room by the moat. Since a guard wasn't patrolling outside the door at the moment, he had little difficulty getting inside. The darkness was smothering. Only the dimmest of light was provided by the stars he could see outdoors. Mr. Smithers felt lonely and upset. Even though he hadn't been captured, he knew he could never leave the castle till his friends were free. Everything depended on him.

He paced about the tiny room, munching on an apple. "Now what do I do?" he thought. "I have to get back to the prisons, but how do I slip past the guards down there? And since I don't have Artemas handy to conjure up some spell, I'll need to get a weapon too. Oh, there are so many details to this job!" He rubbed his whiskers. "It's not easy being a superhero."

Mr. Smithers thought and planned and paced till his brain and feet were equally sore. Midnight rolled around and dawn would soon follow. He felt he had to do something before daylight or else he might not get another chance. Besides, how long could King Rupert and the others survive in that vault with only a limited amount of air inside?

"If only I had taken that troll's club when I took his uniform," he thought with dismay. "Why didn't we think of that?" Then Mr. Smithers stopped fast in his tracks and smiled. He recalled how Artemas had instructed Christopher to prepare the potion that put the troll guards to sleep. "If the boy could whip up a sleeping mixture, then why not me?" With that bit of hope, Mr. Smithers ran off to find the sorcerer's chamber once again.

Because he remembered where the kitchen was located, it didn't take Mr. Smithers much longer to find Malaban's chamber. He entered cautiously. The two trolls that had nearly discovered him, Artemas and Christopher in the curtained alcoves were fresh in his mind. Luckily the chamber was now empty and dimly lit. Mr. Smithers went to the table with all of the vials of colorful liquids and searched through them. He grabbed a blue one.

"Now if I could only remember which color Artemas told

Christopher to mix it with," he wondered. "Was it red or green? With all the commotion from the trolls in the stairway, I seem to have forgotten." Mr. Smithers frantically considered his possibilities. Blue and *red*, or blue and *green*. He desperately wished he could remember. But time was running out, so he grabbed a vial of green liquid and rushed out of the sorcerer's chamber.

Now that Mr. Smithers had some type of defense, his confidence grew. He felt ready to face a whole army of trolls and goblins as he scurried through the deserted castle corridors. Let Belthasar and his men try to stop him. He'd show them a thing or two. But when Mr. Smithers found the door leading to the prisons, his courage started to dwindle at an alarming rate. Once again he considered the possibility that he might make a mess of the situation, or worse yet, get caught. "Enough stalling!" he told himself. "It's do or die time. Smithers, you've made a shambles out of everything else in your life. Do something right for a change! Get on your horse and go!"

Mr. Smithers opened the door and cautiously descended the spiral staircase to the prison. He held his breath as he neared the bottom, listening for any sign of the guards. To his dismay, he heard two voices, the very same goblin and troll that Molly, King Rupert and Ulric had tricked. As he peeked around the curve in the steps, Mr. Smithers could see the guards seated at the table in the guardroom, each munching on a turkey leg and drinking a pint of ale. A ring of keys lay on the edge of the table. He would need those to release his friends.

"Much quieter tonight," the goblin said, smacking his lips.

"Course it is!" the troll replied. "All of the prisoners are locked in the vault. No way they can bother us now. And we've got more ale!" He grinned wickedly, picking a piece of turkey stuck between his teeth. "I'm glad they tossed the princess in with the rest of them. Now I don't have to stand guard over her up in that cold tower."

"Much warmer down here," the goblin said, stretching out his chubby legs. "And good food." He took a gulp of his ale. "No, I don't think there'll be *any* trouble tonight."

"That's what you think," Mr. Smithers thought when hearing the goblin. The thirst for a daring rescue again welled up inside him, so he carefully mixed the blue and green liquids together into one vial. He took a few deep breaths, preparing to spring into action. "Now or never!" he whispered to himself. Then Mr. Smithers ran down the few remaining steps, snarling like a madman. He jumped out of the shadows right into the center of the guardroom. "So you boys don't want any trouble, huh? Well I've got a boatload of it for you! What do your ugly turkey-stuffed faces think of that?"

The two guards nearly fell out of their chairs. "Another one!" the goblin cried. "I thought the boys upstairs caught them all. After him!"

The guards pushed aside their food and jumped out of the chairs, lunging at Mr. Smithers. But he was a split second faster and threw the glass vial on the floor in front of them, shattering it to pieces. "That'll fix you!" he said, preparing to run back up the stairs so he wouldn't feel the effects of the sleeping potion.

To his horror, huge billows of white smoke erupted where the vial had landed, quickly filling the room so that neither Mr. Smithers nor the guards could see a thing. They stumbled every which way, trying to escape from the room.

"What's happening!" the goblin squealed. "I can't see a thing!"

"No kidding!" the troll snapped back. "And stop running into me, you clumsy oaf! Catch the intruder before he wrecks the whole castle!"

Mr. Smithers ignored the rantings of the guards as the smoke continued to billow and grow, now filling up the pantry and slowly drifting through the archway to the cell area. He dropped to his knees and crawled to the guards' table, feeling for the keys on top. He found them. Grabbing the key ring, Mr. Smithers ran in the direction where he thought the archway stood, knocking into one of the guards along the way. He couldn't see which one through all the smoke.

"What a mess I've made," he muttered. "It was blue and *red*, you fool! Not green!"

But there was little Mr. Smithers could do now to change the situation, so he ran all the way down the corridor of cells to the very end. The smoke was less dense here, though it was drifting this way and would soon fill the entire prison. He could still hear the curses and shouts from the goblin and troll, neither yet able to find their way out. Mr. Smithers ignored them when he spotted the iron door. He attempted to open it, trying nearly every key in the lock. Finally the right one fitted, and click!—the door unlocked. Leaving the key in the keyhole, Mr. Smithers grabbed a torch on the wall and rushed down the stairs to the vault below.

"I'll have you free in no time!" he shouted, hoping his friends were still alive, yet knowing they couldn't possibly hear him. The stairs ended and he stood face to face with the vault. Mr. Smithers set his torch against the wall, then grabbed onto the locking wheel of the vault door. He took a deep breath, then started to turn the wheel. He could still hear the shouts from the two guards upstairs, fearing that he wouldn't have much more time.

Summoning all his strength, Mr. Smithers tried to turn the wheel, groaning and clenching his teeth when it wouldn't budge. He thought the vault door had a mind of its own, as if it didn't want to be opened. But Mr. Smithers persisted, and slowly the wheel turned. Little by little the bolt inside the door began to release. He could hear the sound of metal grinding against metal. Just a bit more and he would have it. Then the wheel stopped moving and the door unlocked. Mr. Smithers tugged and tugged at the handle with all his might, till finally the heavy door slowly inched open. He grabbed the torch and walked inside, the pale light faintly illuminating the vault. Mr. Smithers gasped. Not a soul was inside.

"Now that's some disappearing trick if I ever saw one," he thought, stepping farther inside. He scratched his head. Suddenly Mr. Smithers was tackled to the floor by two dark figures.

"We've got him!" one shouted.

"Let's get out of here!" cried the other. "Hurry, before it's too late!"

"Just hold your horses!" Mr. Smithers yelled. "And get off of me! It's Mr. Smithers. Your rescuer!"

The two figures released him and helped him to his feet. "It *is* you!" Christopher said when seeing his face clearly in the torchlight. He and Ulric had tackled Mr. Smithers.

"My stars! So it is," King Rupert said gratefully.

Ulric chuckled. "We thought you were a guard when we heard the door opening. We all hid along the side of the entrance in hopes of surprising you."

"Well you certainly did that!" Mr. Smithers said as he rubbed the stone dust off his pant legs.

"I'm certainly glad you followed us from Endora," Artemas added. "You saved our lives."

"Well I'm glad you're all right and everything's peaches and roses. But you can each thank me later for rescuing you. Right now we have to get out of here!" He looked over the group as they exited the vault and saw that all were in fine spirits, including Princess Rosalind, who had been held captive much longer than the others. Mr. Smithers was honored to finally meet her.

Ulric glanced at the stairs. "I think I hear soldiers above. But what's that?" White smoke began to drift down the steps.

"You do hear soldiers. Two, but there may be more," Mr. Smithers said. "And regarding that smoke, well . . . Let's just say that my plans for a flawless rescue were kind of botched up."

"What went wrong?" Princess Rosalind asked.

"No time to explain, your highness. If we don't leave at once, you might all end up in that vault again. And me along with you!"

Without further hesitation, the seven ran up the stairs into the white smoke. By this time the entire prison level was filled with the billowing clouds.

"Keep together," Ulric said. "If we separate, we'll never regroup in time to escape."

"We might not escape at all!" Christopher said with growing apprehension. "I think I hear a column of guards heading our way!"

His guess proved to be alarmingly correct. The goblin and troll had eventually found their way upstairs and assembled a group of soldiers to stop the breakout. At this moment they were heading under the archway through the blinding smoke, preparing to crush the prisoners in their tracks. There seemed no hope of escape.

"Hide inside the prison cells!" Molly whispered to the others. "Hide inside the cells and let the guards pass by."

All heard the simple yet brilliant suggestion and rushed into the empty cells. And not a moment too soon, for in the next instant a troop of snarling trolls and goblins stampeded by and raced down the stairs into the vault room.

"Now out of the cells and run for it!" King Rupert ordered.

Everyone bolted from their cell and dashed towards the guardroom at the end of the smoky archway. Christopher had an idea at the last moment and spun around to follow the guards to the vault room. He stopped at the iron door and could hear the soldiers at the bottom of the stairs near the empty vault. Christopher called to them. "Hey, you ignoramuses down there!" he shouted, immediately getting their attention. "It was nice visiting you, but the service around here is awful. We're going to vacation someplace else next year!"

The soldiers below were stunned to see the young boy standing in the smoke at the top of the stairs. But before they could rush even a few steps up the staircase to get him, Christopher slammed the iron door shut, turning the key that Mr. Smithers had left there and locking them securely inside.

"That ought to hold those bums!" he shouted in triumph as he ran to catch up with his fleeing friends.

Good luck remained with them as they passed through the silent castle corridors, arriving swiftly and safely back to their hideout. All were delighted to see that Mr. Smithers had a sack of apples and bread scraps to greet them.

"I'm starving," Molly said.

"Just wait a little while longer till we're safely away from here," Ulric said. "We'll leave at once while it's still dark."

Christopher opened the door and everyone piled out of the castle as fast as rats leaving a sinking ship. The cool night air felt wonderfully refreshing. Artemas untied the raft on shore, and he and Christopher pushed it into the icy waters of the moat.

"On board!" The king whispered the order. "Make haste! Make haste!"

In short time, all were safely on the raft—along with the sack of apples and bread—and Ulric swiftly paddled them to the other side of the moat. They had a little bit of trouble climbing back up the steep grassy bank, resulting in a few bruised and dirty limbs. But nobody minded.

When everybody reached level ground, Ulric hurried them across the tall brittle grass to the nearby woods. The stars twirled above as they ran like the wind itself. When they entered the forest, inhaling the sweet smell of pine in winter, their fear and urgency transformed into sheer joy. Molly and Christopher cheered at their escape, and King Rupert cried in happiness that Rosalind stood safely at his side. All were free at last.

CHAPTER FOURTEEN

The Journey Back

Ulric advised King Rupert that it would be best for everyone to stay deep inside the woods on their first mile back, just in case a scouting party should come after them. "Even though we're free, we are still in danger so close to the castle. Besides, the security of the forest will allow us to travel at a slower pace. We can use the extra time to recover our strength."

After marching that long mile through the dark tangle of trees and underbrush, the party was well on the road to recovery from their ordeal. They were in high spirits when Molly suddenly motioned for everyone to keep still. "I hear something moving," she whispered. "Just outside the edge of the trees. Maybe we were followed."

"I hope not." Mr. Smithers wiped his brow. "I've had enough of trolls and goblins to last me a lifetime."

Ulric scouted ahead, hiding behind a tree now and then as he neared the edge of the woods. The starlight shone down on a small grassy opening, and there Ulric saw what had startled Molly. "There's nothing to fear," he called out. "Look what I've found."

Molly and Christopher raced out of the woods first as the others followed. There to greet them was a horse. "My steed!" the king shouted. "So he hasn't abandoned me after all."

"He has stayed loyal to you, as have the other horses. Look over there by those large bushes. I see four others grazing near the stream. I guess they were certain we would come back for them."

"This is the spot where we hid our tents and supplies," Christopher reminded them. "It seems like a week has gone by since we were last here." In reality, their entire adventure inside Malaban's castle had taken only a single day.

The seven retrieved their belongings and were happy to be riding the rest of the way back to Endora. Each rode the same horse as before, only this time Princess Rosalind accompanied her father. "Our mission was an astounding success!" King Rupert declared, congratulating everyone for his part. He didn't speak very much during the rest of the journey home. For in the back of his mind, gnawing at him through every waking hour, was the knowledge that Belthasar still planned to attack his castle in three days.

The return to Endora proved uneventful. The weather grew colder and the dreariness of the dying plains looked as depressing as ever. They slept in the tents for a few hours near dawn, then rose before noon and continued their travels till darkness engulfed them once again. Meals were brief and few. Time dragged on and there was little talk to cheer them. Only after midnight did anyone begin to take heart, for off in the black distance loomed the tiny yellow lights of King Rupert's castle. The weary travelers had finally made it home.

Queen Eleanor greeted the heroes at the castle gate. She embraced King Rupert and cried with joy as Princess Rosalind walked over to her. "My dear!" she sobbed as she hugged her daughter. "I thought I might never see you again."

"I missed you so, mother," she said. "But thanks to these brave people, I'm back where I belong!"

Everyone in the castle celebrated throughout the night, and a great feast was prepared for the travelers. King Rupert and Queen

Eleanor presided over the festivities. Christopher, Molly, Mr. Smithers, Artemas and Ulric were each honored for their bravery and courage during the rescue. King Rupert even knighted Mr. Smithers for his single-handed rescue of the entire party from the vault. The king dubbed him Sir Smithers, the Courageous. Mr. Smithers could find no words to say after the ceremony and merely blushed.

Early the next morning King Rupert called an assembly of all the residents in the castle to inform them of Belthasar's impending invasion. People expressed anger and outrage that another attack was imminent, and King Rupert did all he could to calm their outbursts. One young soldier took the news lightly.

"We defeated Malaban and his troops before. Surely we can do it again when Belthasar arrives."

"I applaud your optimism," the king replied. "But Malaban attacked us with only a portion of his troops. Belthasar is assembling every last soldier he can muster. They will outnumber us by an incredible amount."

"We can go to the surrounding villages for reinforcements," the soldier suggested.

King Rupert frowned. "I have already dispatched scouts to gather help, but that still will not provide us with enough manpower. Every soldier will have to fight two and three times his ability in order to defeat Belthasar."

Queen Eleanor stood to address the crowd. She looked tired and careworn, but an undying strength and determination burned within her. "We face terrible odds. But no matter the outcome, I wish you all the very best. We must stand by our king till the end."

Cheers and applause broke out, but the show of courage on people's faces was overshadowed by despair and doubt in their hearts. Nobody was quite sure what to expect in the days to come.

"If Belthasar leaves with his troops as he had indicated, then they should arrive here in two more days," the king continued. "That gives us little time to prepare. Ulric will propose a plan of action and position our troops." King Rupert went silent and recalled the moment he had found Princess Rosalind safe in the castle tower. How happy he was then, and how terrible things appeared to him now. He cleared his throat to give his final word. "All I ask is that you do your best for the sake of Endora. Dark times are ahead, but may strength and good fortune go with us all." With that, King Rupert and Queen Eleanor left the chamber in silence.

Molly and Christopher had been sitting with Princess Rosalind and Artemas during the king's speech. Ulric had gone off to prepare the battle plans with his officers. Mr. Smithers eagerly followed. Since he had been knighted Sir Smithers, he insisted that he be allowed to help plan for the war too.

"I hope Belthasar and his army freeze on their march over here!" Molly burst out in anger. "I never want to see him again."

Artemas stroked his beard and sighed. "I'm afraid Belthasar will find his way here with little trouble."

"I wish I had locked him downstairs too," Christopher said. "By the way, Artemas. I had nearly forgotten. When will the timedoor reopen?"

The magician smiled. "*I* haven't forgotten. It will open for the last time in two more days. As a matter of fact, on the same day when Belthasar and his army arrive. At least you and Molly will be safely home before the battle begins. But I'm sorry to say that a timedoor will never again connect our two worlds."

The children appreciated the magician's concern for their safety, but could not help feeling guilty that they wouldn't be around to help King Rupert defend his kingdom. "Though I didn't much care for our stay in Malaban's castle, I shall truly hate to leave Endora, knowing I can never come back," Molly said. "It's like a second home."

The two days before Belthasar's arrival passed like wildfire through parched brush. In the early morning hours before the attack, Christopher and Molly waited in Artemas' chamber for the final opening of the timedoor. A warm blaze crackled in the fireplace as the children glanced through a few dusty scrolls to pass the time. They had been virtually ignored ever since the battle preparations began.

The door leading to the balcony was partially open. Artemas could be seen standing out there gazing through his telescope in silence. "What's he doing out in the cold?" Molly whispered to her brother. "It's daytime. Certainly he can't be looking at the stars."

"Don't bother him," Christopher warned. "He's a magician. I'm sure he knows what he's doing."

"I suppose." Molly glanced at the stone wall near the cluttered coat tree. "When is that timedoor going to reopen? We've been waiting here practically forever."

Before Christopher could answer, Artemas rushed inside. "The hour has approached sooner than expected!" he said in a panic. "I must warn the king!" With that, he bolted from his chamber in a whirlwind.

"What was that all about?" Christopher said. "He couldn't have been referring to the timedoor."

Molly shrugged then got up and walked out onto the balcony. A cold dry wind slapped her skin and made her ponytails dance. "I wonder what he saw in his telescope," she said, deciding to take a quick look.

Christopher followed his sister outdoors. "Careful so you don't break it. Artemas would be awfully upset."

"I'll be careful, Chris. Gosh, I'm almost nine after all." Molly looked at the telescope and was puzzled. "I wonder why it's pointing towards the plains instead of at the sky?"

"Take a look," Christopher urged. "What do you see?"

Molly stared into the eyepiece and focused on the brown plains. She saw nothing at first, then was startled when her eye adjusted to the view. "Oh no, Chris! Now I see why Artemas ran out to find the king."

Christopher nudged his sister away to have a look for himself. His jaw dropped in astonishment at what he observed. Miles away on the frosty barren plains paraded forth a huge swarm of trolls, goblins and men on horseback. All the soldiers were armed with swords or spears or clubs. Several of them in front carried red and black banners flapping sharply in the wind. Belthasar led them forth. They numbered over a thousand, grim and merciless, marching straight towards the castle. War had arrived in Endora.

CHAPTER FIFTEEN

The Final Hope

Belthasar's army arrived as the morning sun edged its way above the eastern hills. King Rupert requested a parley with the hostile visitors on the grassy field in front of the castle. With grim faces and heavy hearts, King Rupert, Ulric, Mr. Smithers and four other members of the king's guard waited at the main gate. They watched as Belthasar and six of his soldiers approached the castle on foot. King Rupert and his men then left the castle, walking slowly across the drawbridge to meet with the enemy and discuss their options.

The group of fourteen gathered near a large boulder in the field under the crisp morning sky. Bitter winds cut through their tightly wrapped cloaks. King Rupert finally broke the silence.

"So you have brought your army to my kingdom as promised, Belthasar. Speak quickly! What are your terms?"

Belthasar smiled slyly, his dark eyes burning with disdain for the king. Arga the troll and Crull the goblin stood behind him, equal in their hatred for King Rupert. "You kidnapped our leader Malaban," said Belthasar. "I want him safely returned or I shall order my troops to attack."

"That's preposterous!" King Rupert said. "Malaban made an unprovoked assault on my castle before he disappeared. I had nothing to do with his absence. Now you have the nerve to attack again and demand his return? Outrageous! I have no idea where the scoundrel is."

Belthasar had expected such a response from the king. "If that is all you have to say, then I have no choice but to attack. Unless," he added, with a slight hiss in his voice, "you'd rather surrender at once to avoid a prolonged and ugly battle."

King Rupert knew the odds of winning were against him. His side was highly outnumbered. But he vowed never to give up under any circumstances. "My advisors and I must have time to consider our options," he finally said, hoping to stall for some time.

Belthasar considered for a moment, then nodded. "Very well. I'll give you two hours to discuss matters. If after that time you have not reached a decision, I will order an immediate attack. This is my final offer!" Then Belthasar and the members of his parley team turned and walked back to their troops.

"Quickly! To the castle!" King Rupert said.

Soon they were gathered in the king's chamber to discuss a strategy. "What do you propose?" Ulric asked. "We have enough men to resist a first assault, but after that I fear we cannot hold out for very long."

"I know! I know!" the king wailed. He paced the room and tried to think. "Curses on Belthasar! And double curses on Malaban! Those two have made my life miserable. Oh, if only I knew what to do."

Before anyone could make a suggestion, Artemas entered the room with Christopher and Molly. "The timedoor has reopened," the magician informed the king. "It will remain open for a few hours, then close for the last time."

"I guess this means that you children will finally get to go home," King Rupert said. "I'm sorry that this comes at such an awful time. I had hoped to give you both a proper going-away party. But with Belthasar and his army at my front door, well . . . I hope you understand."

"We do," Molly said.

"Don't worry about a party," Christopher added. "We're just happy that you're going back with us."

"Going back?" King Rupert repeated in surprise. "Whatever do you mean?"

"To find that wicked Malaban fellow," Molly reminded him. "Don't you remember? When we traveled to rescue Princess Rosalind, you promised to go back through the timedoor to find Malaban and bring him back to your world where he belongs." Molly shook her head in disgust. "I certainly hope that man hasn't made a mess of our world."

"He's made a mess of mine!" the king complained. He looked apologetically at the children. "I'm sorry I can't keep my word, but you must understand that there are more important matters at hand. Soon it will be very dangerous in this castle. You two had better return home now while you still can."

Molly's eyes snapped wide open in surprise. "No, sir! We're not going anywhere without you. You led Malaban to our world, King Rupert. Now we expect you to get him out."

"But, Molly . . . !"

"But nothing!" Christopher boiled in anger. "King or not, you can't get rid of us that easily! Molly and I helped you rescue your daughter, and now you just want to send us home like a couple of little kids who are in the way. Well we won't put up with it! Bad enough that we're stuck with Malaban in our world because of you, King Rupert. But now you flat out lie to us by not keeping your word. I don't know which is worse!"

The king was greatly disturbed by the children's remarks. Belthasar had thrown fear into his heart with his threats and his power, but the simple words of these two children cut into his very soul. Deep down King Rupert knew they were right. It was wrong for him to allow the evil sorcerer to poison their world. He realized he would be no better than Belthasar if he let that happen and wouldn't be much of a king. Time was fast running out. King Rupert wondered what to do.

Mr. Smithers finally spoke up after quietly observing for some time. "I believe, King Rupert, that we might have overlooked an obvious solution to our problem."

"Speak up then!"

"You see, sir, if Belthasar demands the return of Malaban in order to call off his attack, then you *should* return through the timedoor to find him. The sorcerer had been hiding out in a cave only a half mile from my diner," Mr. Smithers reminded him. "I could take you there."

King Rupert winced. "Even if I find Malaban and bring him back, and even if Belthasar then calls off his attack, there is still one slight problem."

"What's that?"

"Malaban himself! He attacked my castle once. When he sees Belthasar here with his entire army, don't you think he might want to attack again? I'm defeated either way!"

"Maybe," Christopher said. "But you owe Molly and me your help just like you promised. You may not be better off, but things can't get much worse."

"You've got a point there," King Rupert said sarcastically. Still, he did have to admit that the boy was right. Whether Belthasar *or* Malaban was in charge, his own soldiers would still be badly outnumbered. And since there was absolutely nothing he could do to increase his odds of winning in the next two hours, why *not* try to find Malaban and bring him back? There was nothing left to lose, so King Rupert finally agreed. He would return through the timedoor to keep his word like a king should. He wondered if it would be the last thing he'd ever do.

"This is foolish nonsense!" Queen Eleanor told her husband when she heard the news. She urged him not to look for the sorcerer, but the king convinced her that he had no other honorable choice. With time slipping by like the wind, King Rupert kissed his wife farewell. Then he, Molly, Christopher, Ulric and Mr. Smithers hurried to the magician's chamber where Artemas awaited them. He would go with them on the search too.

"All ready?" the king asked unceremoniously. The pale morning light streamed in from the open balcony door, highlighting the stern expressions on the nodding faces before him. "Then let's get this over with. Artemas, lead the way."

One by one, the six stepped through the wavy distorted section of the stone wall and soon found themselves immersed in starry blackness. The echoing silence of the time passage twirled about and propelled them along. Soon a faint light grew in the distance as they neared the end. Each cautiously stepped out of the timedoor, emerging through the stone wall beneath the bridge by the river. The autumn air warmed them after the chill of Endora. And though the sun had only risen above King Rupert's castle, here it was nearly midnight. The six huddled together in the November darkness as gentle waves lapped against the river banks.

"I expected to see sunshine," Molly whispered. "I forgot, Artemas, that our time doesn't line up with yours."

"How long have we been gone?" Christopher asked.

"About six and a half days according to your clocks," Artemas said. "That's a little over five of our days."

"All well and good," Ulric interrupted, "but we're forgetting our mission. Remember, the timedoor will close for the last time in a few hours. I don't think anyone wants to be trapped on the wrong side after that happens."

"Show us those caves, Mr. Smithers. I want to finish this business once and for all," King Rupert said.

"Let's go to my diner first," he suggested. "My car is parked there. We can drive to the caves and save time."

All agreed, and so they marched along the river till the dreary diner slouched into their view. Rotting leaves littered the outside, and a drainpipe along one edge of the building had fallen down. Molly thought the place looked like a disaster.

"There's a light burning inside."

"I must have forgotten to turn it off when I ran to follow you and your brother through he timedoor," Mr. Smithers said. "The light probably kept away any intruders while I was gone." He looked at his diner and thought the building was in terrible shape, realizing that it was one of the reasons he got very little business. "Though who would want to waste his time looting such a dump," he muttered.

He led the group around the building to his car parked along the side. The rusty green automobile looked as old and unkempt as the diner. Everyone piled inside the car, and soon they were driving off in search of Malaban.

The small caves burrowed into a rocky cliff near the road along the river. The passages inside stretched for several hundred feet, winding this way and that, usually serving as hideouts for children in the summer months. Now the caves lay deserted in the dying days of autumn—or nearly so.

King Rupert inspected the caves in the shadowy gloom. Lanky leafless trees guarded the openings. "They look so morbid," he said. "An appropriate place for Malaban to make his stronghold."

Artemas agreed. "But in spite of the look, we must enter soon. Time is precious. However, we do have the element of surprise on our side."

"Then let's go," Molly urged. "I'm tired of this whole business and am starting to get more annoyed and less frightened with this sorcerer."

"Just wait till you meet him," the king said, glancing up at the stars and shaking his head in dismay. "Very well. We'll go inside. Which cave did he enter, Mr. Smithers?"

"The one on the left," he pointed out.

King Rupert led the way, trudging along the cold leafy ground. Twigs crackled and fallen acorn shells ricocheted sharply against the rocks as they were kicked about. As they entered the cave, the blackness inside was smothering and stale. Each person could barely make out the one in front of him.

"It's like we're trapped inside the vault again," Christopher said, his voice echoing eerily.

"Shhh! Don't say such a thing at a time like this," King Rupert said. "Bad enough we're about to face the sorcerer. There's no reason to bring up the misfortunes we've suffered because of him."

The silence grew as thick as the darkness. Minutes passed like hours. Molly began to think they were lost in their wanderings, when a flicker of light appeared in the distance. As they drew nearer to the light, it grew brighter and painted odd-shaped shadows along the passage. At last the path opened up into a chamber filled with a sickly yellow light from a sputtering fire. The damp air smelled of burnt pine needles and moss. A worn haggard figure sat stooped over the fire, warming his hands. He looked up as the others approached, the firelight reflecting in his eyes. They had found Malaban at last.

Molly gasped when seeing his thin face and blazing eyes, half frightened yet half surprised. Neither she nor any of the others could take their eyes off of him. Malaban seemed to have them under some sort of hypnotic spell. No one spoke a word for the longest time. Malaban finally broke the silence.

"So the great King Rupert has found me at last," he sneered. "You and this ragtag bunch! Why do you bother me in the middle of such a cold and dreadful night?"

"We mean you no harm," Molly said, finding the courage to speak first.

Malaban laughed. "The mighty king lets a child speak for him? Be gone if you have nothing to say!"

"I have plenty to say," the king said after gathering his wits. "I'm here to keep a promise to these children." He glanced at the others for support. "You are trespassing in their world, Malaban. You must come back with me through the timedoor. Any differences we have can be settled in Endora."

The sorcerer stared thoughtfully at King Rupert for a few moments, then started to chuckle. "Your words are quite amusing. Though I despise you and your companions deeply, you *are* very funny." Instantly the sorcerer's mirth changed to a fiery anger. "But enough of this! You have wasted my time for too long already. You know I will not bow to your silly requests. I am Malaban! Now I command you to leave at once before I turn you all into a bunch of sniveling mice!"

Though alarmed at the outburst, they decided to hold their ground. "My king doesn't take orders from you!" Ulric said. "This is not your kingdom, Malaban."

"That's right!" Christopher jumped in. "Who do you think you are? You have no right to order us around."

"Or to turn us into rodents," Mr. Smithers added. "You *were* kidding, right?"

King Rupert stepped forward. "Ignore the comments of the others," he said. "Though I appreciate them greatly, *I* am king, and I alone must settle matters here and now." He looked kindly at Malaban, then swallowed hard before he spoke. "As much as it pains me to admit it, I need your help, Malaban."

King Rupert reluctantly told Malaban about Princess Rosalind's kidnapping and rescue, and how Belthasar at this very moment was poised to attack his castle. Malaban seemed unmoved by the story.

"You certainly are in a fix, King Rupert. But how could I help you?" Malaban snickered. "And why would I *want* to?"

"If you return with us, you can order Belthasar to stop his attack," Artemas pleaded.

"Then I could merely turn around and attack Endora myself," Malaban said with delight. "What an intriguing idea."

"I don't doubt you would," King Rupert said. "But I had hoped we might solve our differences without a battle."

Malaban nodded, adding some twigs to the fire. "Belthasar is a strong-willed soldier. Even if I ordered him to retreat, he might not. But then I come back to my same question—why would I *want* to? It seems that I have you right where I want you, King Rupert, no matter which world I'm in."

Molly couldn't contain her growing anger and marched right up to the fire, glaring at Malaban. "What has King Rupert ever done to hurt you? Leave him and his kingdom alone!"

"Don't snap at me, little girl! I'm liable to turn you into a stone and toss you in the river!"

"Don't ever threaten my sister!" Christopher jumped in. "I don't care who you are!"

Malaban was intrigued by the boy's defiance. "These children are braver than your own soldiers," he said to King Rupert. "Still, they are not strong enough to drive me away from my new home. You must deal with Belthasar as best you can. Though I find it exciting that Endora will be defeated shortly, I am afraid I will have to miss the spectacle. I have my own plans to make here."

"This is treacherous!" the king fumed. "Have you no sense of decency and responsibility?"

"I am responsible to myself alone! I will carve out a new kingdom in this world, and if anybody tries to stop me, he will pay dearly," Malaban snarled. "Now get out of my sight, all of you!"

The world ended for King Rupert at that moment. He knew he must return to Endora soon, only to face the crushing blow of Belthasar's army. His power, his kingdom, and most importantly, his family, would perish in a single day on the battlefield. There was nothing left to do to stop it.

But Christopher had other thoughts. Though despair had claimed the king, he wouldn't allow himself to be pushed around. The boy was in *his* world now, and no one from another world, not even an evil sorcerer, was going to tell him what to do. Christopher kicked a spray of dirt across the fire, making it explode in a burst of blue and yellow sparks in front of Malaban.

"Maybe King Rupert can't get you to call off the attack on his castle, but *I* won't allow you to stay in my world! Get out, you coward!" Christopher pointed to the passage leading out of the caves. Visions of his parents, little Vergil and his home flashed through his mind. He would protect them. "Go back to your own dreary castle where you belong."

"You'd better listen to my brother!" Molly cried, taking her place at Christopher's side.

Malaban jumped to his feet, his face contorted like a wild animal. "You dare call me a coward? A powerful sorcerer?"

Christopher smirked, now less afraid of Malaban. "Yes. You *are* a coward. You're so afraid of facing your own miserable life that you have to wreck everyone else's in order to feel good. Well the world doesn't need people like that. So why don't you just keep your nosy face out of other people's lives and mind your own business!"

Whether Malaban or King Rupert looked more surprised at the children's boldness was difficult to guess. Now the cave was dead silent. No one knew what to do or say at the apparent stand-off, and time was running out. King Rupert glanced at Ulric for advice. Malaban twitched about in uncertainty as the flames of the bonfire snapped.

Suddenly the sorcerer leaped over the burning twigs and stood face to face with Christopher and Molly. "You dare threaten me? Leave now or I'll strike you down with bolts of white fire!" he said with bitterness dripping from his voice.

Artemas and Ulric gasped in astonishment, and Mr. Smithers shook with fear. King Rupert turned ghostly white. "Do as he says! Don't ever cross a sorcerer!"

But Christopher and Molly ignored the king's advice and stood firmly in their places. They stared directly into the sorcerer's eyes, challenging him to do his worst.

"I'm warning you—leave or pay the consequences!" Malaban said, raising his hands above his head as if ready to shoot bolts of lightning from his fingertips. "This is your last chance!"

"Do as he says!" King Rupert said, his knuckles pressed nervously into his face. "Oh please!"

Christopher and Molly didn't move an inch, though Malaban towered above them like a vicious monster out of a bad dream. The sorcerer extended his arms straight ahead, rapidly moved his fingers as if ready to do his worst, and then—his arms dropped lifelessly to his side. Malaban fell to his knees. He buried his face in his hands, sobbing.

"I've lost my powers," the sorcerer whispered. He looked up at the stunned crowd gathered around him. "Ever since I arrived in this world, my powers grew less and less. My magic drained out of me, slowly at first, then much faster as the days went by. I couldn't stop it because the timedoor had closed and I was unable to return to my own world. Now I'm powerless," he moaned, staring helplessly at the children. "And worse yet, I have nowhere to live except for this cold and miserable cave."

Everyone was shocked at the sight of the once-mighty sorcerer groveling before them. King Rupert, realizing he had nothing to fear, was ready to lash out at Malaban. But pity touched his heart as he looked at the tragic figure, and he simply turned away.

"I can't figure it out," Mr. Smithers whispered to Artemas. "I thought this Malaban was so powerful."

"He was. But living in this world seems to diminish one's magic," the magician said. "It happened to me, though I was lucky enough to get home before all of my powers were gone. They have since returned to normal."

"He looks so sad," Molly said. "Will he ever return to the way he was?"

Artemas shook his head, disturbed to see a fellow magician lose his power forever. Yet he knew that Malaban had misused the magic and no longer deserved to possess it. "Once a sorcerer completely loses his magical abilities, they are gone for good, Molly. Even if he returns to our world, Malaban will never regain that strength."

"A shame," Ulric said. "He was once an honorable and loyal magician to his king. What a waste."

Christopher turned to King Rupert. "What do we do with him? We can't leave him here forever."

"I suppose not, even if he isn't a threat anymore."

"We should at least take him back through the timedoor," Christopher said. "I'm sure he'd rather be in his own world, even without his magic."

King Rupert sighed. "I'll take him back, but I'm afraid he'll be of no use in stopping Belthasar from attacking." The king glanced around the cold empty cave, studying the flickering shadows from the dying flames. "I fear that my power will end shortly too. There is no way Endora can hold out against Belthasar. I might as well sit down next to Malaban, for I am surely defeated."

Though they didn't dare speak it, Artemas, Ulric and Mr. Smithers were certain that death and destruction lurked on the other side of the timedoor. Christopher and Molly were equally distraught and felt sorry for King Rupert. All waited anxiously for the king to give the word to depart. Then a frail voice broke the silence.

"Please don't leave. I'll help you—if you let me." Malaban raised his head. His eyes were tired and his face haggard. "I don't want to be left behind. Please take me back, and I will try to talk to Belthasar."

King Rupert spun around and glared at the sorcerer. "Do you mean what you say, or is this some trick? I find it difficult to trust you, even without your powers."

Malaban stood, bent over and shaking. "I am a broken man, King Rupert, who deserves neither your trust nor your help," he said in a strained voice. "But over these last days I have remembered how it felt to be a simple magician, with only my stars and potions and loyalty to my king as my priorities. I once had good in me, and though I can never undo all the evil deeds I have committed, at least let me make some amends," he begged. A tear rolled down his face. "If I return, Belthasar will relinquish his power to me and I will order the army back to my castle."

"You will really do this?" King Rupert asked suspiciously. "As much as I hate to admit it, you are our final hope."

"I give you my word. It may not mean much now, but let me back it up by my actions."

As the king gravely considered the matter with Ulric, Artemas warned him that the timedoor would not stay open much longer. They had to act fast. "Very well," King Rupert decided. "You shall accompany us back to Endora. But we must hurry, as Artemas said. The two hours that Belthasar had granted us are nearly up.

The timedoor will close soon after that. So onward!" he shouted, with a renewed hope. "To Endora! I have one last chance to save my people!"

CHAPTER SIXTEEN

A Flight Through Time

Mr. Smithers parked his car in back of the diner. The doors quickly opened and seven figures climbed out into the still November night. Their shadowy shapes walked to the river bridge as they exchanged whispered bits of conversation. Their frosty breath drifted towards the starry sky in ghostly wisps. Thin winds rustled dried grass and scattered decaying leaves across the landscape.

One by one they stepped through the timedoor beneath the bridge, and moments later found themselves standing in Artemas' chamber as the early morning sun climbed in the wintry skies over Endora. King Rupert immediately rushed off to find his court messengers, dispatching several out onto the field to talk with Belthasar. They were to inform him that a second parley was requested. With that task completed, King Rupert invited his companions and Malaban to his private chamber where they awaited Belthasar's reply. Their hopes wavered on the edge between glorious success and final destruction.

Time still remained in the two hours that Belthasar had given the king. So after receiving his message for another parley, he decided to meet King Rupert in the castle. The messengers escorted Belthasar into the castle in grim silence, taking him directly to the king's chamber.

"Your king is probably ready to surrender," Belthasar taunted. "That will save me the trouble of launching a very nasty battle." He glanced around at the spacious passageways and wickedly grinned. "Very soon this will all be mine. The reign of King Rupert is over."

The door to the king's chamber was open and Belthasar stepped inside. A large crackling fire warmed the room. King Rupert, Artemas and Ulric were seated at a long table along with Christopher, Molly and Mr. Smithers. A few of the king's guardsmen stood at attention nearby. When Belthasar saw their bleak expressions, he felt certain they were ready to surrender. Then he noticed a thin ragged figure huddled next to the king. Belthasar looked closer and gasped.

"You look unsure of yourself," King Rupert calmly remarked. "Is something troubling you?"

"I—I can't believe my eyes!" Belthasar said. The sight of Malaban seated at the table made all of his senses reel. "How can this be?" He cautiously approached Malaban and studied his careworn face. "He is obviously an impostor!" raved Belthasar. "This is some magician's trick to deceive me! You won't get away with it."

"This is no trick," King Rupert assured his stunned adversary. "Malaban has indeed returned."

After a few more moments studying his face, Belthasar grew convinced that Malaban was sitting before him. And though a part of him seemed pleased that his leader was back safe and sound, part of him was also dismayed that he would no longer be in charge of the army of soldiers waiting outside. Belthasar pondered the situation till a faint smile appeared on his face. Perhaps there still existed a way to make his Great Plan succeed after all.

Belthasar rushed to Malaban's side and bowed before him. "I am so happy to see you have returned safely, my leader! Tell me, has King Rupert treated you cruelly during your imprisonment?" Everyone at the table looked appalled at such a statement, but before anyone could refute his words, Belthasar spoke again. "Now that you are free, my great leader, return with me to my camp outside. From there you can command the army I have assembled. Together we can destroy this castle and avenge the evil King Rupert has inflicted upon you! We must hurry!" he shouted, his eyes burning red with rage. "Hurry before the king's guard slay us where we stand!"

Unfortunately for his plans, Belthasar plainly saw that his false warnings did not persuade Malaban in the least. He grew frightened and felt his power slipping away.

"Please have a seat, Belthasar," King Rupert said, offering him a chair next to Malaban. "We wish to talk to you about the current situation."

The peaceful attitude on the king's behalf enraged Belthasar even further. He ignored King Rupert and pleaded with Malaban. "What is the matter, my leader? Have they cast some sort of spell over you? Surely you will not sit idly by and let them take charge over us. We must conquer these monsters while we still have a chance!"

Malaban took Belthasar's hand and shook his head sadly. "Sit," he said. Belthasar, realizing he had no other choice, grudgingly obliged his leader and sat down.

Christopher and Molly watched the proceedings in fascination. Though Belthasar had once proved to be an alarming and outspoken character, he now appeared quite shaken. They couldn't begin to imagine what King Rupert had in store for him.

"Belthasar, your leader entered my chamber out of his own free will," the king said. "He was never my prisoner. And now he wishes to talk to you." King Rupert kindly nodded to Malaban.

"Belthasar, you have always been my most loyal soldier," the sorcerer said in a calming voice. "Though I'm sure you tried your best to run things while I was gone, I have now returned to take over my command. I'm not quite sure of all that has happened in my absence, but you can inform me when we return to the castle."

"Return!" Belthasar cried. "But I have prepared my army— *your army*—to attack! We cannot leave without a battle, my leader."

"There will be no battle," Malaban said. He looked patiently into Belthasar's confused eyes. "I have made some mistakes in the past. There was no need for an attack then *or* now. I have guided you unwisely over the years, Belthasar. It is time we started changing our ways."

Belthasar turned white as the snow, then slammed his fist on the table, startling the others. He jumped to his feet. "How can you say this? How can you do this to me? We will never have total power if we don't attack! It would be a disgrace to withdraw now, to return to our castle like a pack of defeated dogs!"

"Nonsense!" Malaban said, standing and facing him eye to eye. "What reason have we to assault King Rupert's land in the first place?" Belthasar could not give an answer. "Our actions in the past were wrong. So are the plans you have made for this very day. In my desire for power I have done much evil, and sadly I see that I have led you down the same path." Malaban slapped his hand upon the table. "Today all such dishonorable behavior ends here and now! We will retreat to our castle in shame, though much work will be done to make amends. Is that clear?"

Belthasar glared at Malaban, his limbs quivering in rage. All that he had built up was now being snatched away by Malaban. He was not even given a proper chance to explain himself. Belthasar slumped down in his seat, overwhelmed by the defeat served to him. All seemed lost.

"How can you do this to me?" Belthasar said bitterly. "I've kept the troops together in your absence, and now you repay me by crushing my chance for victory." He looked up at Malaban, pleading for a reason. "What made you change, my leader?"

Malaban sighed, rubbing the weariness from his eyes. "I'm not really changing, Belthasar. I'm simply returning to the way I used to be. All the power I had accumulated blinded me to who I really was. I misused that power, and so it was taken away from me. Only then did I realize that I had gone wickedly astray." Malaban looked kindly at Christopher and Molly. "These two children helped me to see the error of my ways. They knew what was right all along."

"Their advice has proved to be most sensible in many instances," King Rupert remarked. "Christopher and Molly will be sorely missed when they return to their world."

Malaban smiled at them then turned to the king. "And now I must return to my own land, King Rupert. I shall order my troops to turn around immediately, and we will never bother you again. I am truly sorry for the suffering we have caused your people."

"Well I am not!" shouted Belthasar, springing to his feet. He rushed to the doorway. "I will *never* return with you, Malaban! Total domination is within your grasp, but you are too foolish to take it. Now you are sentenced to a pitiful existence for the rest of your days," he said with contempt for the old man. "I will fend for myself from now on, but I promise you this. One day I will rise again to power and crush you all!"

Belthasar rushed out of the chamber with a shrill laugh and slammed the door. Before the king's guards could reach him, Belthasar pulled out a dagger at his side and lodged it underneath the door to jam it shut. Then he bounded through the castle corridors and disappeared.

King Rupert signaled to his guards. "Get that door opened at once! Then have a search party track down Belthasar. As long as he is on the loose, he is still a menace!" The guards charged at the door till it burst open, then chased after Belthasar. King Rupert then turned to address Malaban. "Now, my friend, we must deal with the army gathered outside my castle. I won't believe this ordeal is over till I see every last soldier marching back across the plains. And soon!"

A short time later, as King Rupert had wished, Malaban stepped out onto a balcony overlooking the brown fields in front of the castle. His soldiers below were amazed to see their former leader standing there. They cheered at his return, then eagerly listened as he told them about his change of heart. "There will be no war against these lands!" he loudly proclaimed.

Many of the troops shouted in delight, for the idea of another battle had grown distasteful to them during their cold and tiring journey to Endora. Most of the men wanted only to return home in peace and wait out the winter months in their own castle. Many panicked though, especially the scores of trolls and goblins who were loyal to Belthasar. Ever since he had appointed two of their kind to be leaders, the trolls and goblins hoped to secure a castle of their own someday. Now their eyes widened in terror as their plans for conquest disintegrated in front of them. Many fled across the plains into the neighboring mountains and forests and were never heard from again.

Malaban left the castle soon after, promising there would never be another war between the two kingdoms as long as he ruled. "Though my time as a leader will be short," Malaban added, much to King Rupert's surprise. "I will return to my castle only long enough to undo the damage I have caused there and in the surrounding villages. At the same time I will send out several scouts to locate King Alexander, our true leader whom I shamefully banished into the wilderness."

"He has not been heard from in years," King Rupert said. "What will you do if you find him?"

"I will surrender the castle back to King Alexander upon his return, and then await my punishment as he sees fit. I deserve no mercy from him."

King Rupert couldn't believe the words he was hearing, yet told Malaban he was doing the honorable thing. He expressed hope for a future filled with peace, then bid him farewell. Slowly Malaban climbed onto his horse and led the remaining troops back to his castle. His soldiers trudged silently behind, weaving their way across the grassy plains like a dark strip of ribbon caught in a breeze.

"I shall send an envoy to Malaban's castle in the spring," the king said to Ulric as Malaban departed. "Though by then it may be King Alexander's castle once again. I'll be curious as to what changes the months will bring to those lands." He sighed and walked back to the castle. "Now there's only one piece of business left. We must hurry. Time is scarce."

That final piece of business concerned Christopher and Molly and their return through the timedoor. The children gathered in King Rupert's chamber for a hasty farewell. Also present were Queen Eleanor and Princess Rosalind, along with Ulric and Mr. Smithers. Molly asked why Artemas wasn't there.

"He's in his chamber keeping an eye on the timedoor," King Rupert said. "He will be here shortly. In the meantime, I'm afraid we must say our good-byes. I'm sorry circumstances didn't allow us to give you a proper farewell party," he said teary-eyed.

"Now that the time has arrived, I am sad to be leaving," Molly said. "I feel as if I've spent half a lifetime in your world, yet not enough time to really get to know it."

"I'll miss it too," Christopher said solemnly. "If only the timedoor didn't have to close forever. Then Molly and I could visit you whenever we liked."

"You were here when we needed you most," King Rupert said gratefully. "You helped me save my daughter. I can never repay you for that."

"Neither can I," Princess Rosalind said. She knelt between the children and gave them each a tender kiss on the forehead. "My brave young soldiers! I shall miss you both."

Queen Eleanor dabbed a tear from her eyes. "We are indeed thankful," she added. "More than you could ever know. So if there is anything we can do for you before you go, please name it."

Christopher and Molly blushed at the honor bestowed upon them, but declined any gifts. "We have traveled to a new world and lived out adventures others only dream about!" Christopher said. "What else *could* we want?"

"You are wise to treasure those experiences," Ulric said. "They will serve you well throughout life."

"I'll certainly have wonderful stories to tell all my friends," Molly said. "And even to little Vergil. Oh, I do miss him and my parents." Then Molly looked up at Mr. Smithers standing behind the king's chair. "And what about you, Mr. Smithers? Are you glad to be returning to your diner? I remember how puzzled you looked on that Saturday morning we all barged into your place for hot chocolate," she laughed. "King Rupert was as jumpy as a cricket!"

Mr. Smithers looked at the children with a mix of joy and sorrow. "I'm afraid I won't be returning through the timedoor with you. I've thought about it a lot and have asked King Rupert's permission to stay here in Endora."

The children couldn't believe what they were hearing. "If you stay, you'll never be able to return to our world. The timedoor will never reopen," Christopher said.

"I know, but I've thought about my decision very carefully," Mr. Smithers replied, trying to sound cheerful. "Life just suits me better here. There's nothing for me back home except that run-down diner. And that's not worth the nails that are holding it together. Besides," he added, hoping to erase the frowns from the children's faces, "I am a member of the king's royal guard. I was dubbed Sir Smithers, remember? How could I possibly leave now?"

"I remember," Molly sadly replied. She ran over and hugged him. "I hope you're happier living here. I'll miss you," she said as tears welled in her eyes. "I'll miss all of you a whole bunch."

Christopher and Molly went up to each person to make their final good-byes. The pain they felt was the worse they had known since arriving here. Yet each knew that a part of them would for-ever remain in Endora.

Artemas rushed into the room moments later, announcing that the timedoor would soon close. With King Rupert's blessing, the magician escorted Christopher and Molly out of the chamber as the others looked on in silence. Mr. Smithers waved a clumsy good-bye, and Queen Eleanor wiped away another tear streaming down her face. Christopher tried to smile as he headed out of the door. Molly simply waved her fingertips. "So long," she said, her voice cracking. Then she followed her brother out of the room.

King Rupert could only watch as his youngest traveling com-panions disappeared from his view. No words could express his sorrow and loneliness at their departure, so he closed his eyes and said nothing.

Artemas quickly led the children back to his chamber. Though he too was sorry to see them depart, Artemas knew he couldn't delay very long to tell them so. "There isn't much time. A few minutes at the most," he informed them as they rushed up the stairs to his chamber. "After that, the timedoor to your world will be closed for good. It may be months before conditions are proper for me to create another one. And who knows where *that* one will lead."

"I'll miss you," Molly said.

"We both will," Christopher added. "Thanks for dropping in on our world."

"It's been a pleasure," Artemas replied.

As the trio raced down the passageway leading to the magician's room, Christopher recalled the moment when he and Molly first stepped foot into the corridor. How frightened and excited they had been. Now all their fears had vanished to be replaced with an empty and gnawing sadness. He would truly miss the place.

"I guess we'll be home in time for breakfast," Molly said when seeing the door to the magician's chamber at the end of the passage. "As sad as I am at leaving, it'll be good to get back. My garden must be overgrown with weeds by now!"

But visions of her pretend garden quickly vanished as Molly screamed in fright. For at that moment Belthasar jumped out from a side corridor, landing directly in front of the door to the magician's room. Christopher, Molly and Artemas stopped dead in their tracks.

"So you can't wait to go home!" he snarled at the children. Belthasar rubbed his hands as he inched closer to them. "Well you better get used to this cold and miserable place, because you're *not going home!*"

The children backed off in fear. Artemas leaped in front of

them to confront Belthasar. "How dare you threaten these children. Get out of my sight before I call the king's guards!"

"Go ahead! By the time they find me I'll have gotten what I came here for." He glared at Christopher and Molly. "To keep those two from ever returning home!" Belthasar laughed viciously. "So you thought you were on your way home without a care in the world. Well *I* don't have a home now, thanks in part to you two! You helped convince Malaban to ruin me! Now I'll never rule again. But you didn't care because you thought you were going back home. Well let me tell you, little urchins, that's no longer the case!"

"We didn't do anything to hurt you!" Molly snapped. "We just helped Malaban get his life in order."

"And you seem to need the same help," Christopher said. "Big time!"

"Don't tell me what I need!" Belthasar cried in a frenzy, attempting to grab the children. But Artemas blocked his way. "All I know is that you two destroyed any chance I had for power, and you'll pay dearly for that! You'll never return to your home, do you hear me? Never! Never! Never! You will remain stranded in this world for as long as you live!"

Belthasar's eyes flashed in rage as he lunged at the children. But Artemas saw this coming and plowed into Belthasar, throwing him against the wall. The magician quickly opened the door to his chamber and ushered the children inside.

"Flee while you have the chance!" he cried. "The timedoor is beginning to close! Run! Run! I'll take care of Belthasar!"

Christopher and Molly watched paralyzed in fright as Artemas wrestled to keep Belthasar from entering the room. The two fought in the corridor like wild animals. Christopher finally snapped to his senses and realized time was running out.

"Hurry, Molly! I can see the timedoor starting to fade. We have to leave right now or we'll never get home!"

Molly glanced at the wall by the coat tree and knew her brother was right. The waviness around the edges of the timedoor had begun to solidify into solid rock. "Then let's go!" she cried, grabbing Christopher's hand. They ran towards the wall and jumped through the timedoor, leaving Endora forever behind them.

"You won't get away that easily!" Belthasar shouted from the corridor as he struggled with Artemas. With one final howling surge of strength, he shoved Artemas to the floor and freed himself. Belthasar bolted into the magician's chamber and slammed the door shut.

"Come back!" Artemas cried as he struggled to his feet. "You may be too late!" But his warning was in vain. Belthasar had already leaped through the timedoor.

Stars danced wildly in the black space surrounding them. Christopher and Molly ran through the time passage using every ounce of strength they possessed. Finally they saw the lightness of the exit looming ahead. But it too had started to vanish. The edges were solidifying.

"I see the other end!" Molly said, very much out of breath. "But it's fading! We're not going to make it!"

"Yes we will! Run faster!" Christopher said, tightening his grip on his sister's hand. "Run as fast as you can!"

They ran swiftly till their legs burned in pain. Then their fears instantly multiplied when they heard Belthasar far behind them, but getting closer by the second. "You'll never escape me!" he cried madly. "I'll pursue you forever! Do you hear me? Forever!"

"He's gaining!" Christopher shouted. "He's only a few strides behind! Just a little farther to go!"

But when Christopher and Molly felt they couldn't run another step, they found themselves emerging through the stone wall underneath the bridge by the river. The cold autumn air awakened a new energy inside them.

"We're home, Chris! We're home!" Molly cried with joy, hugging her brother.

"But we're not safe yet!" Christopher said. "Keep running! Belthasar is right behind us!"

So they raced along the leaf-covered road by the river, afraid even to glance back at their pursuer. Suddenly a sharp clap ripped through the air, nearly throwing the children to the ground. The sound of rock slapping against solid rock rang in their ears. A bloodcurdling scream echoed from within the stone wall under the bridge—then all was dead silent. Christopher and Molly cautiously walked back into the shadows beneath the bridge. The stone wall was again solid rock. Belthasar had not been quick enough. The timedoor had closed forever.

CHAPTER SEVENTEEN

Back Home

Christopher and Molly dropped to the ground, exhausted and in shock. "Is he gone?" Molly asked after resting for a few moments. "I heard Belthasar scream, and then—"

"He's gone," Christopher said while staring at the bridge. "He won't trouble anyone ever again." He stood and brushed off his clothes then gazed up at the stars. He guessed that it was well after midnight. "We better head home, Molly," he said, offering his sister a hand to help her up. "We've been away long enough."

Molly nodded. "That was the longest week of my life. I'm glad to be home," she said, relieved that Endora was now far away. Yet a sense of sadness overcame her at the same time, for she knew she could never return. "Do you think King Rupert and the others miss us already?"

"Maybe. I miss them." Christopher sighed and kicked a stone across the road. "But I suppose we'll both forget everything that happened over time. We'll never get to go back. It's not fair."

"I certainly won't forget!" Molly insisted. "Not if I live to be a hundred years old. So much has happened to us, Chris. How could we forget?"

"I don't know," he muttered. "Let's just go home."

The two started to walk along the road to their house, leaving behind the bridge, the diner and the river. But they hadn't gone more than a few yards when a dark figure starting rushing towards them. Christopher feared that Belthasar had somehow escaped, so he grabbed Molly's hand, preparing to run off in the opposite direction. Their alarm quickly vanished as they saw their father approach.

"Daddy!" Molly cheered as she and Christopher ran to him. "I missed you!"

Mr. Jordan hugged his children, not ever wanting to let them go. He looked at their grinning faces, laughing and crying at the same time. "If I weren't so happy right now, I'd scold you two for certain," he said, hugging them a second time. "Where have you been, as if I didn't know?"

"We were with King Rupert and Artemas in Endora," Christopher said. "Didn't you find the message I wrote on the stone wall under the bridge?"

"Your mother and I found the note when we returned to the diner. She was hysterical when realizing you went through the timedoor," he said. "Worst of all was knowing that we couldn't follow you. The door had already closed." Mr. Jordan took them each by the hand and continued to walk home. "What did you do in Endora for a whole week?" he eagerly asked.

"You'll never guess in a million years!" Molly challenged.

Christopher and Molly took turns explaining every detail of their adventure, from the journey across the plains to their imprisonment in Malaban's castle, and especially Princess Rosalind's rescue. Mr. Jordan was particularly moved when hearing about Malaban's turn from evil and Mr. Smithers' decision to remain forever in Endora.

"You'll have to tell the story all over again from the very beginning," Mr. Jordan said. "Your mother and little Vergil will want to hear every detail."

Soon they arrived at the house amid a bluster of swirling leaves. Warm yellow light shone from every window. Mrs. Halloway's barn stood silently in the dark field across the road. Mrs. Jordan greeted Christopher and Molly with abundant hugs and kisses, and even a slight scolding, though the children knew she really didn't mean it. Little Vergil jumped up and down at the sight of his long-lost siblings, shouting with joy till they had to calm him down with stories of their travels.

While they talked around the kitchen table, Mrs. Jordan treated everyone to hot chocolate and toast with grape jam. Molly insisted that she had never tasted such delicious jam in all her life. Her mother agreed, then told Molly that the jam had been made from the grapes Artemas had grown in their own living room.

"That seemed like ages ago," Molly said. "I'll miss Artemas so much. And King Rupert too. He's the first king I've ever met."

"And probably the last one," Christopher said sadly. "Just when we found the greatest playground in the whole universe, it's taken away from us. Playing in that old barn won't be half as fun compared to sneaking around a huge castle or riding horses across the starry plains. It just won't be the same."

Christopher felt quite glum when going to bed that night. Endora seemed like a dim memory as he drifted off to sleep. Now more than ever, he felt certain that he and Molly would slowly forget about King Rupert as the days drifted by. But the outlook grew brighter the following morning at the breakfast table. Mrs. Jordan walked into the kitchen carrying a small bundle and set it on the table. Christopher and Molly smiled in astonishment.

"I don't think any of us will ever forget about your visitors from Endora," their mother assured them, holding up two objects. Shining brightly in the morning sunlight were King Rupert's sword and crown that she had hidden down the cellar in the apple sack.

THE END